"Buona notte," he whispered,
"buona notte, carissima."

He took her in his arms and kissed her . . . How ordinary, commonplace a kiss it seemed . . . And why must she still remember Enrico's touch? Ursula's heart beat with rage. Yet even as she raged, she realized the anger was meant for herself. What made her respond so utterly to the arrogant Enrico? Her reason told her she was much better off with his brother, Lorenzo. Did sense and sensuality . . . have to be as different as pleasure and pain?

Bantam Circle of Love Romances
Ask your bookseller for the books you have missed

Dear Friend,

Enter the Circle of Love—and travel to faraway places with romantic heroes . . .

We read hundreds of novels and, each month select the very best—from the finest writers around the world—to bring you these wonderful love stories . . . stories that let *you* share in a variety of beautiful romantic experiences.

With Circle of Love Romances, you treat yourself to a romantic holiday—anytime, anywhere. And because we want to please you, won't you write and let us know your comments and suggestions?

Meanwhile, welcome to the Circle of Love—we don't think you'll ever want to leave!

Best,

Cathy Camhy
Editor

CIRCLE OF LOVE™

The Botticelli Man

Alexandra Blakelee

BANTAM BOOKS
TORONTO · NEW YORK · LONDON · SYDNEY

THE BOTTICELLI MAN

A Bantam Book/May 1982

*CIRCLE OF LOVE, the garland and the ring designs are
trademarks of Bantam Books, Inc.*

ISBN 0-553-21515-9

Published simultaneously in the United States and Canada

—————————————————————————————

*Bantam Books are published by Bantam Books, Inc. Its
trademark, consisting of the words "Bantam Books" and the
portrayal of a rooster, is Registered in U.S. Patent and
Trademark Office and in other countries. Marca Registrada.
Bantam Books, Inc., 666 Fifth Avenue, New York, New York
10103.*

—————————————————————————————

PRINTED IN THE UNITED STATES OF AMERICA

0 9 8 7 6 5 4 3 2 1

One

His dark, almond-shaped eyes stared into her own, and she thought he was the most beautiful man she had ever seen. Even when she turned away, she could still feel his bold gaze; an intense yet tender look that had captivated her from the start. His brow was wide and untroubled, his nose classic but not so classic as to be sharp. Her grandmother would have pegged him as an aristocrat for his nose alone. And his mouth—here was a mouth made for kissing, almost heart shaped but for the corners, which were drawn slightly downward.

"Why are you so sad, my love?" Ursula murmured, gazing into his brown eyes.

"*Attenzione,* you dreamer—the gallery's closing."

"Is it really that late?" Ursula put down her paintbrush and turned to meet Paola's grin.

"I'm sure Botticelli would have been flattered by your devotion, but what about my brother? Vincenzo trails after you, a slave of love, and you're

1

so besotted with a Renaissance portrait, you don't even notice."

Ursula laughed and began to pack up her paints. She had long ago ceased to be embarrassed when Paola caught her drifting off into the fifteenth century, entranced by the model in *Portrait of a Youth.* "Aren't you exaggerating?" she asked, thinking that it was this Italian flair for grand gestures, this gift for theatrics, so different from her own subdued New England character, that she loved in her friend.

"Not a bit," Paola assured her, stepping back to study Ursula's painting. "I also don't exaggerate when I say your reproduction is very good, *buonissimo.*"

"Do you really think so?" Ursula tried to look at the portrait objectively, but all she saw was the penetrating, inexplicably exciting gaze of a familiar stranger. "Let's get some lunch," she said, turning away abruptly, amused by what Nana Willa had always called her "excessive imagination."

Leaving the Borghese Gallery, the two young women strolled through the park. It was a sunny, lazy Roman afternoon. Children in blue school smocks gathered around a Punch and Judy show; lovers, spending the siesta together, embraced in the shade of trees.

"Bella! Bellissima!" The young men who followed Ursula and Paola were loud and boisterous in their praise. It was Ursula Stewart, tall, green-eyed, with straight blond hair falling halfway down her back, who drew the most attention. All her features set her apart as a foreigner, but she had never felt herself a stranger in Rome. The warmth of the Italians enveloped her, giving her comfort and a sense of belonging.

The Botticelli Man

Ursula's mother had died of rheumatic fever shortly after she was born. Shattered by his loss, Samuel Stewart, a professor of archaeology, had given up his chair at Harvard and, taking his infant daughter with him, wandered from one archaeological dig to another. "I don't understand you, Samuel," the imposing Willa Stewart would complain during her son's brief visits back to Boston. "Your ancestors went to a great deal of trouble to settle this country, and there you are roaming about like a rootless gypsy. I won't have my granddaughter growing up in those great holes with only a bunch of bones to play with. She needs a woman's care, the company of other children."

When Ursula was twelve, Professor Stewart finally capitulated and sent her to spend the winters on Beacon Hill. She attended Miss Peabody's School for Girls, took tea with her grandmother at the Copley Plaza, and accompanied her to the afternoon concerts at the Gardner Museum. Pleasant though this life was, Ursula would wait impatiently for summer, when she could once again join her father in Egypt, in Greece, or Jordan, where he was unearthing the ancient city of Jericho. She became an accomplished linguist, could adapt to the customs of any country, but it wasn't until she came to Rome to study art that Ursula felt truly at home for the first time.

Paola Santini was a fellow student at the Belle Arte and Ursula's best friend. Small, with olive-colored skin and jet black hair, she was high-spirited, mischievous, and very protective of Ursula.

"Let's eat here, shall we?" Paola said as they came to an outdoor café surrounded by leafy green trees and the white stone busts of ancient Roman generals and poets.

3

"Perfect," said Ursula, who never tired of the way Rome combined its history and art.

"By the way," Paola said, once they had sat down and ordered, "I told Vincenzo to pick you up tonight at eight."

"Do you know what a bossy sister you are? Not to mention friend."

"Yes, of course," said Paola, imperturbable. "And after dinner the four of us will go to a poetry reading, did I tell you? A friend of Alberto's is reciting his work."

Ursula folded and refolded her paper napkin, wishing she could care for Vincenzo the way Paola did for Alberto. The last few times they'd been alone together, Vincenzo had been too quiet, too attentive, on the verge, she knew, of blurting a declaration she didn't want to hear.

"Well?"

"It sounds like fun." Ursula hesitated. "And you know how sweet I think Vincenzo is but—"

"It's all right, it's all right," Paola assured her. "He knows that you only like him as a friend. He's happy just to be in your company. But you—what more are you looking for in a man? Vincenzo's handsome, intelligent, and witty."

"And your brother, don't forget that," Ursula added, laughing.

As they sat, lingering over their lunch, she only half listened to Paola, allowing her thoughts to return to the portrait of the handsome youth in the Borghese Gallery. The mystery that surrounded him had become an obsession with her. Who had he been? Where had he come from? Nobody seemed to know or, for that matter, care. The portrait's interest for others lay in the fact that it was painted by Sandro Botticelli. "The model was one of many aristocrats who had the good fortune of being made immortal by Botticelli," Professor Armado had said. "I'm afraid that is his significance to us, and that alone.".

Evening church bells were ringing by the time Ursula's last class ended. With damp cloths she carefully covered the bust she was sculpting. It was to be a surprise for Nana Willa, who still complained of not seeing enough of her wandering son. When Professor Stewart had stopped in Rome on his way to a dig in Egypt, Ursula had dragged him to the Belle Arti, sat him down on a stool in a deserted studio, and begun to punch at a great slab of clay. Now, almost two months later, she could see her father coming to life: his unruly mane of hair, the finely chiseled cheekbones that were in such contrast to a strong, stubborn jawline.

After so many hours of quiet concentration, the city streets always gave Ursula a moment of pleasant disorientation. No matter how tired she felt, she needed only to walk down a narrow cobblestone alleyway to find herself replenished. Muscles stopped aching, her mind cleared as she saw a small fountain, a courtyard, or even an illusive color that she wanted to capture. But there was no time for that tonight, she reminded herself, crossing to the bus stop; Vincenzo would be coming to collect her in an hour's time. Suddenly the weariness returned, and she wondered if it simply was the idea of Vincenzo that made her tired.

From the bus window Ursula looked out at the shops they passed, chic boutiques with the latest fashions from Milan. A lavender bikini caught her eye, and she decided she'd ask Paola to come shopping with her on Saturday. The bus stopped next to the Majestic Cinema, where the new Fellini film was playing, and Ursula, craning her neck to see the billboard, gasped in disbelief. There, on the crowded sidewalk, was her Renaissance man. It wasn't possible. But that face, she knew it as well as her own. The bus jolted forward, and though she pushed her way to the back window for another glimpse of him, he had vanished. It must have been a trick of her imagination, she told herself, an apparition. Yet she could have sworn she had really seen him.

When she got off the bus, Ursula paused a moment to look at the distant Colosseum—its timeless columns standing high and strong in the night. A single star was shining over its center.

"Star light, star bright. . . . I wish it really had been the Botticelli Man," she murmured, half mocking herself for her superstitious games. She walked past the sunken ruins of the Roman Forum and turned onto her street.

Via Bacino, the "Street of the Little Kiss," a tiny narrow sienna-colored passageway, could hardly have been more different from stately Beacon Hill.

"Ciao, signorina."

"Buona sera."

Neighbors and shopkeepers, lingering in their doorways, greeted Ursula effusively, as though they had not seen her that same morning. "How are you, signorina?" called the old man who sold milk at the *latteria*, as did the woman sweeping the entrance of the wine shop.

"Signorina Stewart, signorina!" Maria, the portiere of Ursula's building, ran out into the courtyard waving a letter. She was a short, round woman, as kind as she was curious. "It's a letter from your father. Good news, I hope?"

The Botticelli Man

My darling daughter, Ursula read as she climbed the four steep flights to her apartment:

It was a joy to hear from you. The Botticelli project sounds fascinating, although I must confess that I am not familiar with the portrait. You so piqued my curiosity, however, that I made what inquiries I could of my esteemed colleagues. Old Professor Smith tells me the painting once caused quite a stir in the art world. It was apparently first attributed to Andrea del Castagno, then to Piero di Cosimo and to Ghirlandaio and even Pollaiuolo. Finally it is thought to be the work of Botticelli—if indeed it is. You can see how the question of the painter's identity has touched the archaeologist in me. Much as the subject of the painting has so obviously touched the artist in you. I am quite well—in Cairo for a few days to pick up some supplies. Our work goes slowly, and I doubt I shall get away for a visit in the spring. But I trust you'll be coming here in the summer. I love you and anxiously wait for more news.

Love,
Papa

An image of the Botticelli Man standing in the crowd flashed back into Ursula's mind as she put the letter away. But this was no time for fantasy, she scolded herself, and reality meant taking a shower and dressing in the next fifteen minutes.

The apartment was small but so well arranged one didn't notice. The large main room had bookshelves, plants, and a bed covered with an Abruzzi blanket of blue and green. Two bright Indian tapestries hung on opposite white walls, and several large pillows meant to replace armchairs were scattered around the room. The hooked rug partially covering the red-tiled floor had been a gift from Nana Willa, who insisted Ursula would catch pneumonia without it. French windows overlooked the busy street, and between them was a drawing board with a high stool.

Ursula took a hurried, uncomfortably tepid shower. Wrapping herself in a huge towel, she made up her face. The mascara she put on made her lashes look so long and thick they might have been false. She outlined her green eyes with a black pencil, accentuating their size and color, and was still trying to decide what to wear when the doorbell rang.

"I'll be there in a minute." She threw on a kimono and opened the door to the dark, slender young man who stood there. "Ciao, Vincenzo." Guileless, unaware of the charm of her disarray, Ursula kissed him Italian style on both cheeks. "Well, are you just going to stand there staring at me while my neighbors stare at you?" she asked, suddenly self-conscious, trying to keep the annoyance out of her voice.

"I hope I'm not too early," Vincenzo said, following her into the apartment.

"No, it's me. I'm late as usual." Already she was feeling that odd guilt he inspired. "I'm sorry Paola made you come all this way to pick me up."

"Oh, but I wanted to. Anyway, I was in your neighborhood getting my motorcycle fixed."

She smiled. "Not again? Poor Vincenzo. Well, help yourself to some wine. I'll be ready in a minute."

But when Ursula returned five minutes later, dressed to go, she found that it was her portfolio Vincenzo had helped himself to.

"Do you know him?" she asked, an overpolite tone

covering the anger she felt at seeing him handle the Botticelli Man.

Vincenzo colored and cleared his throat. "Should I?" he asked, not meeting her gaze.

She took the painting from him. "Only if you're a Botticelli fan—that's his *Portrait of a Youth.* It's my project this semester."

"I thought it was somebody you knew. It's so lifelike—it's awfully good." Vincenzo's voice had softened with relief.

"No, it isn't. Not yet." Ursula replied, and firmly returned the canvas to the portfolio—her secret bond with the Renaissance Man safe again.

Parioli, where the young Santinis lived, was on the other side of Rome. Her hair blowing wildly, Ursula held onto Vincenzo as he weaved his Triumph 800 in and out of the evening traffic. They finally pulled to a screeching stop in front of a modern apartment building, where the scent of lilacs and honeysuckle lay like a thick mist on the warm night.

Paola, clucking like a mother hen, hurried from kitchen to dining room and back again. "You're late. And it's such a good dinner. We need time to enjoy it. Always late, Ursula, like a typical artist."

"And you"—Ursula laughed, taking the salad bowl from her—"what are you?"

"Oh, Paola—she's so practical and down-to-earth she forgets she's an artist. Isn't that right, Vincenzo?" said Alberto, who sat on the sofa watching the familar scene with amusement. Half-German, half-Italian, Alberto was a short, husky young man with bright blue eyes and reddish-blond hair. He and Paola had been together for over two years. It was a stormy romance, filled with tempestuous fights. "What can we do?" Paola would shrug. "He's a writer, and I'm a painter. We both have the classic artistic temperaments. When we fight, we fight with fury but later. . . ."

"Take more, more," Paola told Ursula.

"It looks like marvelous cannelloni."

"Well—it isn't. It's pasta al forno."

Alberto winked. "That's what these Sicilians call cannelloni."

Paola turned on him. "And where would an Italo-Hun like you have eaten such a cannelloni? You see how many layers of pasta there are? And prosciutto? And hard-boiled eggs?"

"I see a very nice cannelloni."

Ursula, light-headed from the red wine, giggled with Vincenzo, until finally taking pity on Alberto, she asked what time the poetry reading would begin.

"In half an hour," he replied gratefully. "We really ought to be going."

While Alberto and Vincenzo went to get their bikes, Paola and Ursula picked lilacs and tucked the blossoms behind their ears and in whatever buttonholes they could find.

"Eh, Vincenzo, look at these delightful flower children," Alberto leered, driving up onto the sidewalk.

"Help, Ursula! I think some Hell's Angels have found their way to Rome, and I fear for our virtue." Paola laughed, then hopped onto the back of Alberto's motorcycle.

"Wait," Vincezo called to them. "Where are we going?"

"Just follow us," Alberto called, disappearing around the corner.

Vincenzo tried to keep up but was stopped by a red light. By the time the light changed, the motorbike had stalled. There was no sign of the others, and he pulled over to the curb.

"Bloody bike. Now we've lost them. I'm sorry."

"It doesn't matter," Ursula said. "We can go to a place near my apartment. Someone's always reciting poetry there."

A stairway led below street level to the Camilla Café, a favorite haunt of students and artists. The tables and the slightly crooked benches were made of rough, unpolished wood, the walls painted a warm burnt-orange color. Ursula and Vincenzo found a place in a corner of the crowded dimly lit tavern.

"I guess there's no poetry tonight," she said, smiling at him, hoping, that despite the candlelight, the effect was sisterly.

Vincenzo looked into her eyes, but before he could speak, the waiter came with wine and olives, and, to Ursula's relief, a young bearded man began to play the classical guitar, his music hypnotizing the room into silence.

Later, as they stood in the courtyard of Ursula's building, Vincenzo said, "May I come up and talk to you for a moment?"

Ursula hesitated. "Yes, of course. We'll have some coffee."

Upstairs, she set the espresso pot over a low flame and then joined Vincenzo in the other room.

"Have you started studying for your orals yet? Or don't they have oral exams in medical school?"

He ignored her questions. "Ursula, do you have any idea how I feel about you?" he asked, taking both her hands in his. "I'm in love with you." His voice was low and husky, and endearments rushed out, almost incoherently. "I love you," he repeated, and taking Ursula in her arms, he kissed her hungrily, so lost in his own desire that it took him several moments to realize that she was fighting him.

"No, Vincenzo. Stop it!"

He let go and stared at her with glazed eyes.

"Listen to me, I'm not in love with you. You're a good, dear friend, and I love you as that, but only that. I never meant to give you any other impression. Please understand me. Please be my friend."

There was a long silence, and Ursula watched Vincenzo anxiously as he paced the room composing himself, picking up the pieces of his pride.

"Very well," he said at last, staring out the window. "Of course, I'll be your . . . friend. I'll always be your friend."

He left after that, abruptly, and a moment later Ursula heard his bike screeching off into the night. She sat very still, clenching and unclenching her pale hands. What's wrong with me? she asked herself. Vincenzo is bright, good, and sensitive. Everything Paola says he is—but I feel nothing when I'm with him. I look at a picture of a nameless man who lived over five hundred years ago, and I feel shivery. Suddenly smelling something burning, she ran into the kitchenette. The espresso pot was burned through.

Two

The next morning Ursula arrived at the Borghese Gallery just as it was opening. She paused in the main hall thinking it was more than the colored marbles and frescoes that attracted her. There was an aura to this Renaissance villa that soothed her very soul.

"Buon giorno, signorina," the little white-haired museum guard said, taking Ursula's easel out of the cloakroom. "You're early this morning."

"It's never early enough."

"You artists." He gave her a look of sympathetic respect. "You work like field hands. I hope you remember to stop for lunch today."

"I will." Ursula laughed.

But in fact, had it not been for the arrival of a large guided tour of German tourists, she would not have noticed the time. The morning had vanished—it was already well past noon. She stepped back from her canvas noting all the minute discrepancies.

13

Well, eventually she'd get it right. But now the dull ache in the small of her back and her stiff neck warned Ursula that it was time for a break. There was just enough time before Professor Armado's lecture to get a sandwich and the new sable paintbrush she needed. She packed up her gear and, portfolio under arm, lingered a moment longer in front of the *Portrait of a Youth*, staring into those eyes that returned her gaze, that seemed to look at her with recognition.

The best art supply shop was in Trastevere, the old, picturesque artists' quarter on the other side of the Tiber. At Piazza Santa Maria, the heart of Trastevere, Ursula stopped at a little café to buy what Paola called a schoolboy's lunch, a thick, crusty square of white pizza filled with ham. Taking it outside with her, she slowly walked around the piazza, delighting in the way the café's bright umbrellas formed a half-circle around the fountain and at the way the sun sparkling on the water was reflected in the gold mosaics of the church. Children ran between wandering tourists, continuing, uninterrupted, their game of soccer.

"Oh, my God," Ursula said, or thought she said, and felt her heart skip a beat. It was the Botticelli Man again. He was sitting at an outdoor restaurant, the white tablecloth and bread basket giving a solid reality to the Renaissance face above them. Had he been draped in purple velvet and trimmed with ermine, she could not have been more stunned, more certain that she had conjured him up, feature by feature, from the fifteenth century. That aristocratic nose, the imperious arch of the eyebrows, that sad, sensual mouth. Ursula stood transfixed, portfolio under her arm, purse dangling from one hand, the forgotten pizza in the other. His eyes, those deep brown eyes she knew so well, boldly met her own, and only the hot afternoon sun assured her that it was daytime, that this was no dream.

"Ciao, lady." A motorcycle with two boys veered by, one of them snatching the purse from her slack grip.

"No, stop!" Ursula gave a startled, ineffectual cry.

Several men started running after the motorcycle, and through the crowd gathering round her, Ursula saw the Botticelli Man leap onto another motorcycle and speed away.

"You're American, no?"

"They got your handbag?"

"Did they take all your money?"

"Never mind a foreigner's handbag," shouted a wild-eyed young man, pushing into the crowd. "That fellow stole my motorcycle."

"Stupido—who'd want that old wreck?"

"Look, the gentleman's coming back."

The crowd parted as the Botticelli Man rode up and nodding, returned the motorcycle to its owner, the handbag to Ursula.

"You should be more careful, miss," he said in perfect English. "It's dangerous to stare at strange men." The full mouth she had painted that very morning turned up in a charming smile. "Especially when your handbag is hanging in midair."

"Thank you," Ursula murmured, blushing yet unable to stop staring at him.

"We have met somewhere before?" he asked.

Ursula lowered her eyes in confusion. "No, no, we haven't." To regain her composure, if not her dignity, she spoke in Italian. He must understand that she was not just another tourist. "I'm sorry I was staring—I didn't mean to be rude. It's only that you remind me so much of . . . somebody."

The shadow of a frown appeared on his forehead, but he smiled. "Now I shall be rude and ask whom?"

"Oh—just a friend." A weak lie, Ursula knew, but things were embarrassing enough without dragging the truth into it. "Well, thanks again, so much." She started to give him her hand, remembering only just in time the pizza it still held, and giving a nod that she hoped was graceful enough to redeem the whole gauche scene, hurried away.

But who was he? Where had this Botticelli Man come from? The furious dialogue Ursula had with herself lasted the entire bus trip back to the Belle Arte. What a fool she had been to run away from him like that. She didn't even know his name. Yet she could scarcely have gone on standing there. For all his politeness, there was something reserved about him—almost arrogant. She flushed at the memory of her awkwardness, not daring to interpret that look in his eye. Had it been interest or only amusement?

"During his brief career, Raphael painted more than forty Madonnas, in which he developed Leonardo's classic pyramidal composition." Short, stocky Professor Armado paced the length of the classroom. Ursula's eyes were riveted to him, but her mind remained on the Botticelli Man. The way he had leaped to her aid had definitely been the act of an old-world cavalier. She smiled, recalling the incongruity of his sitting astride that battered old motorcycle in his impeccable beige business suit.

"Please make note," Professor Armado was saying, "that Raphael's *La Belle Jardinière* is an example of a simple design serving as a vehicle to express both the religious and the human value of the relationship of the figures."

Ursula reached down to get a notebook out of her portfolio and only then realized, with a sinking heart, that she must have left her portfolio in Trastevere. Vaguely she remembered propping it against an empty café table during the excitement over her purse being snatched. But she couldn't leave in the middle of a lecture. Surely a waiter would find it and keep it until she got there. Asking the boy next to her for some paper, Ursula took notes mechanically, anxious only for the class to end.

For once, Professor Armado finished on time. Forgetting her promise to meet Paola, Ursula raced down the hall, bolting out of the Belle Arte building. As she started to cross the street, the door of a parked car suddenly flew open, blocking her path.

"Watch what you're doing," she cried furiously, then stopped in astonishment when she saw it was the Botticelli Man.

"Please get in," he said, leaning out of the chauffeur-driven black Mercedes. "I've been waiting for nearly an hour."

"But how did you find me?"

"You forget what a small town Rome is, Signorina Stewart. Come." Grabbing her arm, he pulled her into the car. "Don't look so frightened," he said, laughing. "I'm not kidnapping you, I assure you." He held out his hand. "I am Enrico Benvoglio. So you see—you are not getting into a stranger's car. Now, tell me: do you always go about losing things?"

Ursula smiled with relief at the sight of her portfolio. "I'm afraid I've kept you busy picking up after me today."

"My reward," the Botticelli Man said, still holding her hand, "will be your company at dinner."

"Yes, of course." He smiled, and she wondered if she had replied too quickly.

"So that's settled. Now I shall take you home."

"Thanks. I suppose I'd be quite capable of losing

my way next," Ursula said, and was rewarded with a laugh that showed his slightly uneven, very white teeth.

The Mercedes smoothly maneuvered its way through the narrow streets. The windows were shaded, and for the first time Ursula felt cut off from Rome. Intoxicated with the car's smell of new leather and with Enrico Benvoglio's musky cologne, she had no idea where they were, nor did she care.

"I took the liberty of looking at your work while I was waiting for you. That portrait—your friend, perhaps?" He stared at her, his brown eyes almost hard in their intensity.

She blushed, not knowing if he was mocking her. "It's Botticelli's *Portrait of a Youth*. But you probably know that. It's incredible—how very much you resemble it. That's why I was staring at you in the piazza, of course."

His expression softened. "The portrait comes to life," he said. "And will return at eight." The Mercedes had stopped in front of her building. "Arrivederci."

Ursula stood watching the car disappear around the corner. It was amazing the way the Botticelli Man made her feel—so light, gay, and yet tentative, as though her feelings were no more than a handful of bright balloons that might at any moment burst. . . .

The telephone was ringing when she opened the door.

"What happened to you?" Paola demanded.

"I'm sorry I didn't wait. I couldn't. I left my portfolio in Trastevere at lunchtime. Just got back this second."

"Oh, no! Did you find it?"

"Well, let's say it found me." Ursula paused. "It's a little complicated."

"Complicated? Aha! That means a man."

"Well, yes, sort of." She was somehow reluctant to talk about him. "Listen, I've got to go now. We'll talk tomorrow, okay?"

Ursula put down the phone feeling a pang of guilt at having cut the conversation short. But how crazy it would have sounded to say, "Guess what—I've just met the Botticelli Man." And she must stop calling him that—he had a perfectly good name of his own. "Enrico Benvoglio," she murmured aloud, savoring the sound of it.

For over two hours Ursula tried on and discarded clothes, searching for the right thing to wear to dinner. Clearly that sleek Mercedes was not going to deliver them at a neighborhood trattoria, the kind of casual restaurant she usually went to. The navy blue suit had a nice cut, but she looked too like Willa Stewart's granddaughter, dressed for tea at the Copley. And the golden caftan her father had sent from Egypt turned her into a harem girl. In the end she put on a simple black sheath and then, thinking it too plain, tried to choose between several necklaces. But she couldn't concentrate any longer. It was nearly eight o'clock, and she was remembering the strong grip of Enrico's hand as he had pulled her onto the car, the odd excitement she had felt.

When the bell rang, Ursula looked into the mirror a final time, grabbed a white rope shawl from the closet, and ran downstairs.

"You look beautiful," Enrico said, helping her into the car.

"So do you."

He laughed. "Thank you kindly, sir."

Ursula blushed as she realized what she had said. But he did look beautiful in that brown velvet suit that so exactly matched his eyes.

"I'm taking you to my favorite restaurant. Well,

one of them. It's outside of Rome, so we might as well start with cocktails now." He mixed two drinks from a small, well-stocked bar, then picking up the intercom phone, said, "Tomaso, we'd like some music."

"Bach, isn't it?" Ursula said, leaning back to listen to the soft, sweet sonata. "And my favorite."

"Mine, too. Do you like your drink? It's a sort of champagne cocktail of my own invention. My friends call it ambrosia—why are you smiling?"

"I was thinking how appropriate: the drink of the gods, this winged chariot—"

"Ah, yes, it's a bit what you would call Hollywood-ish, no doubt. But, in fact, this car is as mundane as any other office. My business involves frequent trips. But I want to hear about you. You speak Italian very well."

"Thanks to my father, I teethed on languages." She told him about her nomadic childhood until, realizing finally how loose her tongue had become and that she had been hearing only the sound of her own voice, she stopped.

"Please go on."

"The rest you already know. I'm here in Rome studying at the Belle Arte. And that's all."

Enrico smiled. "I find that hard to believe. A beautiful woman like you doesn't spend her nights alone studying."

"I have friends," she said lightly.

"More than you know," he replied, raising her hand to his lips.

The car stopped as Ursula finished her second champagne cocktail. "If your noble intention was to ply me with drink, you've certainly succeeded." She stood breathing in the fresh night air. Far in the distance she could see the lights of Rome, like stars on the horizon. The sky, too, was filled with stars; they had never looked so close and large.

As if sensing her thoughts, Enrico said, "They say no wrong is ever done here because the stars keep watch over everyone. This restaurant is called Stella d'Oro—'Golden Star.' Very apt, isn't it?"

Bathed in the light of many candles, the restaurant was indeed a golden star. Crimson velvet drapes covered the windows, tall cushioned chairs encircled tables laid with silver and decorated with vases of fresh flowers.

But Ursula's surprise at this lavishness was nothing compared to hearing the headwaiter say, "Count Benvoglio, welcome."

She stole a glance at Enrico. But of course. She ought to have guessed. Nobility was in his every look and gesture.

"I'm sorry, Count," the waiter was saying. "We weren't expecting you tonight. It will be a few moments before your table is ready."

"Si, si," Enrico said curtly. "We'll wait in the bar."

"You didn't tell me you were a count," Ursula said, as they sat in the elegant bar and Enrico ordered champagne.

"Oh, it's not such an unusual thing in Italy." He smiled, but there was pride in his voice.

Ursula held up her glass of champagne. "It seems everything here is gold."

"You most of all," Enrico said, and gently raising her chin, he looked into her eyes. A long searching look that was as intimate as a kiss.

"Your table's ready, Count." The headwaiter led them to an alcove at the far end of the restaurant. After filling their glasses with more champagne, he loosened the velvet drapes, leaving them in complete privacy.

"Now it's your turn to tell me about yourself," Ursula said.

Enrico gave her a teasing smile. "I'm like any other Renaissance youth. My family has several estates that I look after. It's not the most amusing dinner conversation."

"Tell me about your parents." She wanted to know everything about him. She wanted to read him as she would a book.

"They stay in the country most of the time, either in Sicily or at their villa outside of Rome. They are, I think you would say, rather proper and predictable."

"Do you have any brothers or sisters?"

"Yes," Enrico said. Then, "Do you like oysters?"

"Anything," Ursula replied. "Everything."

The headwaiter served them himself: succulent oysters baked on a bed of sea salt; this followed by a silver platter of shellfish—shrimp, crayfish, clams, mussels, and lobster in a rich garlic sauce.

"Enough, please," Ursula finally pleaded, setting down her fork.

"Not yet. Nobody leaves my table without dessert."

Ursula laughed. "You make me feel like I'm back at Miss Peabody's school."

"Heaven forbid." Enrico stood up. "Come, I'll show you this is no Miss Peabody. We'll have coffee on the terrace, and you'll see how the moon shines on our hills."

Later as they were driving back to the city, Ursula said, "How lovely it was out on that terrace."

"Ah, but you should see where my family lives. Perhaps one day you will."

"Perhaps," Ursula echoed, trying to match his casual tone. "Where is it?"

"By the sea—a small village called Circeo."

They drove on in silence and then, musing aloud, Ursula said, "Strange, isn't it, to think that we only met today."

Enrico looked amused. "But we've known each other since the fifteenth century." Gently he took Ursula in his arms. His kisses were unlike any she had ever known, tender but sure.

"You'd best go inside now," he finally said, his low, soft voice another caress.

Ursula sat up, realizing with embarrassment that they had arrived at her building, that the chauffeur was sitting still, his back stiff and discreet.

Enrico kissed her lightly on the forehead. "I'll call you tomorrow. Buona notte, carissima."

Three

"I can't believe you finally have a free hour for an old friend," Paola told Ursula as they strolled along the Tiber with their sketchbooks. "If poor Vincenzo knew, he'd be here like an Olympic runner with his torch."

Ursula gave her a sidelong glance to make sure this was only a good-natured gibe, for there was truth to what Paola said. In the last few days Enrico had either appeared at the Borghese Gallery to take her to lunch or, in the late afternoon, had been waiting outside the art school. The evening before, he had sent his chauffeur with a note instructing her to meet him at the opera. And if his manner was a little too peremptory, too casual, she would find a warmth in his deep brown eyes, a certain tender note in his voice, that more than made up for it.

"And where is the Botticelli Man today?" Paola was saying.

"He had to go to Sicily rather unexpectedly. A business trip, I think."

"What, by the way, is the count's business?"

It embarrassed Ursula that she still didn't know. "I'm not sure. He manages his family's estates—perhaps that's all. He doesn't talk much about it."

"Aha—a man of mystery. That's always seductive, isn't it?" And then, in an uncharacteristic moment of seriousness, Paola added, "Maybe I'm going to sound like my mama, but the truth is you don't know any more about this Botticelli Man than you do about the one hanging in the Borghese Gallery. Are you sure you're not just falling for a Renaissance face—and a title?"

Ursula smiled. "They're just fringe benefits."

"Well, if you ask me, cara mia, I think you're being swept off your feet."

In the week that followed, Ursula more than once asked herself if indeed she was not being swept off her feet. There was something disturbing to her in that phrase—the suggestion that she no longer had any will of her own. Yet at the same time she couldn't deny the new excitement Enrico had brought into her life.

Dearest Nana Willa,

How I wish I could describe what Rome is like in the spring. *La primavera* they call spring—"the first truth"—and it is! The city is even more beautiful than its pictures. Definitely more than mine, but perhaps spring fever has been interfering with my work. This evening, for instance, a friend of mine took me to a concert—Berlioz's *Symphonie fantastique.*

When the "Songe d'une Nuit du Sabbat" began, I closed my eyes and thought back to when I was six inches shorter, six years younger and by your side. Oh, Nana, I do wish you'd come to Rome. It has everything you love so much in Boston and more. After the concert we took a lazy carriage ride through the park and ended up sitting by the Trevi Fountain, watching that baroque fantasy of gods and steeds, who seem to be moving through the rushing water.

I'm sure by now you must be wondering who this friend of mine is. Let me introduce Count Enrico Benvoglio, a handsome young *gentleman*, who this very same evening has invited me to visit his parents' villa in Circeo. Just think of it—your granddaughter making her debut into Italian nobility.

Goodnight, dearest Nana, goodnight.

Love,
Ursula

The next morning Ursula called Paola from the Borghese Gallery. "Oh, I'm so glad I caught you. Listen, I'm just leaving the gallery. Can you meet me at my place for lunch?"

"Of course. But that breathless American accent of yours tells me I'm being invited for more than a meal, right?"

Ursula laughed. "Right. I was going to tell you when I saw you—Enrico's invited me to his parents' villa for the weekend. They're very proper, he says. What does that mean? I've absolutely no idea what clothes to take, I probably don't have anything right. Do you suppose they think all artists are bohemians?"

"Calma! Tranquilla! Help's on the way."

Ursula had nearly forgotten that there was nothing in her little refrigerator but some milk and half a cantaloupe. Silly fool, she told herself, the weekend's nothing to be so nervous about. It's hardly a command performance at Buckingham Palace. Anyway, no time to worry about it now. Paola's going to expect more than half a cantaloupe for lunch.

She stopped at the grocery to buy prosciutto and salami, hurried on to the cheese shop where she picked out a fresh, damp mozzarella, and at the bakery quickly gathered some warm, crisp rolls.

"So this fascinating man actually has parents?" Paola said later as they were eating lunch.

"What a cynic you are."

"I'm not. I'm a worrier."

"What's to worry?"

"I'm not sure—maybe nothing, maybe everything."

Ursula looked at her. "What's that supposed to mean?"

Paola put some mozzarella on a roll, then said, "Maybe it only means that I could trust my little brother with you, but this count? What do we know about him? He sounds too good to be true." She took a bite. "So where is this villa?"

"In Circeo—a rather grand one, and I don't mind telling you *that* makes me nervous."

"And so it should. Didn't Enrico tell you that Circeo is named for the witch Circe, who turned Odysseus' men into swine? Let's hope the mother countess doesn't follow suit. And speaking of suits"—Paola grinned— "shall we have the fashion show?"

The girls quickly finished eating, then ransacked two closets and a storage trunk before they made the final choices for the weekend. There was a beige linen suit for the trip down, a long, green, silk-jersey gown for dinner, a flowered Laura Ashley dress for Sunday, and a white trouser suit neither one of them could decide to leave behind.

"Bless you," Ursula said, throwing her arms around Paola. "You're an angel for helping me pack."

"Yes, well, next week it's going to be your turn. The newspaper is sending Alberto to Germany for a couple of months, and I've decided to go with him."

"Oh, no. Why didn't you tell me?"

Paola laughed. "I haven't exactly had the chance."

"But what about school?"

"I'm going to ask Professor Armado for a leave of absence, or whatever it's called."

"Oh, Paola, I'll miss you."

"And I you, amica mia."

Promptly at three, just as Enrico had promised, the black Mercedes arrived.

"Signorina, your friend is here," Ursula's neighbors shouted up from the street.

"Il conte é arrivato!"

Ursula hurried downstairs, but this time it was the chauffeur who stood waiting for her. Enrico was sitting in the back of the car with his briefcase open, immersed in work.

"Ciao, bella," He gave her the perfunctory Italian greeting, barely glancing up. "You'll have to forgive me—these papers must be dropped off on our way to Circeo. Shall I ask Tomaso to put some music on? It won't distract me. Or perhaps you'd rather read? The magazines are in the side pocket."

Ursula checked her disappointment. This was hardly the greeting she had anticipated. Taking up a few magazines, she began to leaf through them disinterestedly. Midway through a monthly journal dedicated to social gossip, she suddenly stopped, stifling a gasp, as she saw a large photograph of Enrico, a beautiful woman on either arm.

MAN ABOUT TOWN

Count Enrico Benvoglio, one of the most handsome and eligible bachelors of the season, caused quite a stir at the Principessa Alessi's twenty-first birthday party. Two of Rome's well-known beauties, Stephania Pettini of Pettini Oil, and Teresa Guilio, daughter of producer/director Giancarlo Guilio, photographed above with the count, are said to be in strong competition. Will he stay a bachelor for much longer? Our sources tell us that recently he was seen vacationing in Positano with still a third possibility—the gorgeous French actress, Genevieve Delcroix. The count, when asked if marriage bells were ringing, said, "Perhaps they are but not for me."

Feeling a sharp pang of jealousy, Ursula slammed the magazine shut. Enrico, still working, was oblivious to her presence, let alone to what she was reading. Just as well—she didn't want to talk. Paola had been right. She really knew nothing about him, this "Man about Town."

"You're not too bored, darling?" Enrico murmured. "I'm almost finished."

Ursula shrugged. She was not going to be another one of his darlings, thank you very much. Moving away, closer to the window, she stared out at the countryside—groves of olive trees with leaves shining like silver in the sunlight; golden haystacks shaped like houses against a tranquil blue sky. Perhaps she was being childish to get so upset by a scandal sheet—and an old one at that. Of course Enrico had known other women, and, yes, beautiful ones. But *she* was the one he was taking to meet his parents.

"Finalmente. And not a moment too soon," Enrico said, snapping his briefcase shut as the Mercedes turned down a narrow dirt road. "Sorry for this little detour, but my business here won't take much time. And you," he said, reaching over to take Ursula's hand, "you, I think, will especially appreciate this beautiful estate."

They drove through a large park of elms, cypresses, and myrtle, in whose shade stood neglected statues, empty fountains, and ivy-covered pavilions. In the distance was the outline of a villa, a massive, dignified country house, whose long, porticoed arms reached out as if to enclose the garden.

"A Renaissance building," Ursula said, forgetting everything but her pleasure in what she saw.

"Yes, part of it. When I was a child, this was truly a splendid place. It's sad to see it so run-down now." Enrico drew her closer and smiled. "Perhaps I shall buy it one day and restore it to all its former glory."

Looking at his dark, lustrous eyes, Ursula thought of the Botticelli portrait, and it did not seem surprising that Enrico should feel an attachment to this Renaissance manor.

"I won't be long," he said as the car stopped in front of the villa.

Half an hour passed. Impatient and restless, Ursula helped herself to a Cinzano from the car bar. She wished Enrico had taken her along, business or no. Well, it was too lovely to just sit here waiting. She rapped on the chauffeur's window. "Tomaso, I'm going for a walk in the garden."

"As you wish, signorina."

The sun was setting as Ursula crossed the vast lawn. Bright orange streaked with yellow blended into bold crimson over the horizon. Her hand itched for a brush. There was a bowerlike pavilion at the bottom of the garden, and wandering over to it, Ursula was startled to find an elderly woman draped in layers of black lace sitting there.

"I hope you realize you're trespassing."

"I'm so sorry," Ursula said. "I'm a friend of Count Benvoglio. I thought I'd wait for him here."

"Ah, the count. Forgive me. There are so many tourists who wander through my gardens uninvited."

"I guess his business is taking a little longer than he expected."

The woman laughed. "You'd better settle down for a nice long wait, signorina. Gambling always takes longer than one expects. If you're enjoying the sunset, I'm sure you'll be thrilled with the dawn." Pulling a mantilla over her head, she turned her back, signifying the end of the conversation.

Gambling? What an odd thing to say, Ursula thought, walking back toward the villa. But the woman had probably been thinking of other days. A bit mad, no doubt.

"So there you are," Enrico said, waiting for her by the car. "I was afraid I'd lost you."

"Not quite yet," Ursula teased, getting into the backseat beside him.

Circeo was still several hours away, and Enrico, more relaxed now, told her stories about the medieval hill villages they passed.

"How can you remember so much history?" she asked, impressed and amused by the flow of these tales.

He gave her his most disarming smile. "What I don't remember, I invent."

Toward the end of the trip, Ursula dozed off, her head on Enrico's shoulder.

"We're almost there." He gently kissed her brow, her cheek, and Ursula felt as though she were waking to a dream. "Look, down there, those lights on the shore—that's Circeo. I think we'll stop in the village for dinner—it's already so late—and you'll love our local restaurant."

Mamma Alfredo's was deserted except for a few fishermen. The proprietress, Signora Alfredo, shook Enrico's hand warmly, then took them to a little table in front of a blazing fire.

"Here we eat family style," she told Ursula, giving her a huge smile. She went away but quickly returned, bringing them large steaming bowls of fish soup and a plate of fried garlic bread.

"You like it?" Enrico asked. "Have you ever seen such big mussels?"

It was the first time Ursula had seen him like this, so relaxed and gay. He seemed younger here—less aloof, less enigmatic. As they ate, he talked easily, entertaining her with more stories about the area.

"You have missed my cooking, eh?" The signora beamed as she cleared the empty plates and set down a dessert of peeled peaches in white wine.

"Always, Signora Alfredo," Enrico told her.

"I'm so glad you asked me to Circeo," Ursula said, reaching impulsively for his hand. "I hope your parents will like me."

He gave a surprised look. "You needn't worry about that."

* * *

The Botticelli Man

As the Mercedes followed the winding coastal road, Ursula watched the lights of the village disappear. She wondered if Enrico's parents would be waiting up for them. How much easier to meet them in the morning when the she felt rested.

"The estate begins here," Enrico announced calmly, as they passed through a gateway onto a narrow sandy road.

Ursula wondered how he could sound so calm. She herself had stage fright, and there was no pretending she didn't. Nor was it any help to remind herself of prominent Beacon Hill. There was no comparing *The Mayflower* to centuries of Roman nobility—no matter what Nana Willa said.

"Take a good deep breath," Enrico said, opening his window. "We're driving through the orange groves. A pity it's so dark, but you'll get a better look in the morning."

Ursula could see the white villa now, illuminated by ground lights. Built on a hill, it commanded a view of the ocean and seemed to her as elegant and glittering as a small palace. They turned into a long, curving driveway lined with gracious statues, then stopped in front of the villa.

"Come along," Enrico said, "Tomaso will see to our bags."

"Welcome, welcome," a small crone of a woman cried, running to meet them and grabbing both Enrico's hands.

"Pina, hello, old thing. This is Signorina Stewart. She comes all the way from America."

"I am honored to meet a friend of the count's."

"Pina is my old nurse," Enrico said. "She used to chase me through the orange groves."

Pina gave a big toothless grin. "Oh, yes, he was a little devil. Here, Count, give me your briefcase. I will carry it for you." She led them into the house. "And how are your dear parents?"

"Quite well, thank you. Still in Switzerland, but I think the countess is getting bored. They'll be returning soon, no doubt."

Ursula stopped short. His parents in Switzerland? Her bewilderment turned to anger.

"We won't be wanting breakfast before ten," Enrico was saying to the old woman. "I'll take the briefcase upstairs myself."

He guided Ursula up a gracious marble stairway, and she felt her arm stiff and unyielding beneath his hand. Why had he lied to her?

"I hope you like your room," Enrico said, showing her into a luxurious bedroom. The white ceiling was high and had a gold-leaf border. Blue brocade drapes covered the windows, and large bouquets of fresh flowers filled the room with a rich, sweet perfume. The large canopied bed was on a dais, its blue silk curtains loosened, and the satin covers turned invitingly down.

"Like?" Ursula echoed coldly. "How not?" Turning away she saw his dark, handsome face reflected in a huge golden mirror. Never had he looked more like the Botticelli Man. But no, she quickly corrected herself, this was the "Man about Town," Rome's favorite playboy. And did he bring his little starlets here, too? Or was this suite reserved for naive American tourists?

"What are you thinking? You look upset."

"I am," she said, her gaze as direct as her words. "You told me we were coming to visit your parents."

"But I never said that," Enrico replied, giving her a puzzled frown. "I said we were coming to their villa."

Ursula stood by the door waiting for him to leave. "Well, Enrico, it's been a long day. . . ."

"It certainly has," he said, taking off his jacket.

"How I welcome the weekend." He began to unbutton his shirt. "Would you like a nightcap?"

"What I would like," Ursula said, opening the door, "is for you to leave."

Enrico raised a perplexed eyebrow.

"You said this was my room."

"For heaven's sake, Ursula, what's come over you? I thought you wanted to spend the weekend with me."

"I did." She looked at him, her green eyes steady and grave. "But not like this."

"My dear girl." Enrico gave a curt laugh. "It would have been difficult to guess *that*."

"If you're not leaving," Ursula said, wounded by this barb, "I am," and she ran down the hall.

"Just a moment. Wait!" Enrico called after her, but she did not look back. Propelled by hurt and anger, she flew down the stairs and out the door, colliding with the chauffeur.

"Oh, Tomaso. Listen—that restaurant—I have to go back there now, at once."

"Very well, signorina. Tell the count I'll get the car out again."

"The count will not be joining me."

The chauffeur nodded, expressionless. "Very well, signorina."

Signora Alfredo was closing the restaurant when Ursula burst in.

"My mother's ill. I must get in touch with friends in Rome—I have to get back." A wild torrent of lies tumbled out.

"Poor child, calma, calma. The telephone is in the kitchen. Come."

It wasn't until Ursula heard Paola's phone ring repeatedly that she realized how late it was.

A sleepy voice finally answered. "*Pronto?*" It was Vincenzo.

"I'm sorry, calling this late. It's me, Ursula. Is Paola there?"

"No, she isn't home yet. Is anything wrong?"

"Everything. I'm ringing from Circeo, a restaurant called Mama Alfredo's. Please, can you come and get me? I'll explain later."

"I'm on my way."

So that was that. Ursula put down the phone and rested her head on the table. Damn Enrico and damn her naiveté. For it was true, he hadn't ever actually said that his parents would be there, that he wanted them to meet her. She had assumed it. Still, he had let her go on assuming it. Why hadn't she guessed that all he wanted was a little weekend fling? How matter of factly, how casually, he had brought her to that beautiful bedroom . . . beautiful, yes, like a courtesan's parlor.

Signora Alfredo came into the room and stroked Ursula's hair comfortingly. "Hush now," she crooned. "Crying isn't going to make things any better."

It was nearly two o'clock in the morning when Vincenzo arrived. "Ciao bella," he said, as though there were nothing untoward in her midnight summons.

"Ciao," Ursula replied, taking great comfort in his easy manner, the friendly kiss on her cheek.

"I brought you Paola's leather jacket—it's a little chilly. But the bike is behaving admirably."

The night had turned misty, hiding its stars. The motorcycle raced along the coastal road, and Ursula's long hair blew wildly in the rush of the wet, salty wind.

"Are you all right?" Vincenzo shouted.

"All right," she called back and resting her head

against his back, watched the waves breaking in the moonlight until she could no longer see or smell the ocean.

Four

The next morning Ursula slept late. When finally she did wake, scenes from the day before came crowding back into her mind—Enrico's gay laugh at supper, contrasted with his cold, opaque stare as she fled from the bedroom. Resolutely pushing these memories aside, she dressed quickly, took her portfolio, and hurried to the little café on the corner.

It was as familiar and cozy here as her own kitchen. The cappuccino that the proprietor set before her was always just right—rich and frothy, with chocolate and cinnamon sprinkled on top.

"Will you come out with me tonight?" he asked, as he did every morning.

"Sorry, but I have a date."

He shrugged. "It doesn't hurt to ask. One day I might get lucky."

"How lucky is that?" His wife teased, setting down the tray of pastries she had brought in from the kitchen and tweaking his ear.

The Botticelli Man

Though it was by now after eleven, Ursula lingered over her breakfast, finally admitting to herself that she simply didn't want to go to the gallery, had no more desire to see the portrait than the man. Was it too late, she wondered, to change her semester project? She ordered another coffee and took the painting out of her portfolio. Almost flinching under the dark, penetrating gaze of the Botticelli Man, she studied the canvas. But she must finish it—one didn't abandon art because of a playboy count. And if the Renaissance youth's face held a hint of that same arrogance, it was of no consequence to her. In fact, now that she could see the painting dispassionately, perhaps she would do a better job. Tomorrow she'd get back to work on it. There were too many other things to do today. The apartment, for instance, was a mess.

The portiere, surprised to see Ursula, ran to meet her in the courtyard. "Oh, signorina, a gentleman left a suitcase here for you."

"Grazie. Was there any message?" she asked, in spite of herself. Apologies, she knew, were hardly the count's style.

Maria shrugged. "I don't know. I was at the market, and the gentleman left it with my grandson, who left it with the signora next door when he went to his soccer game." She paused for a breath. "Is everything all right, signorina?"

"Everything is just fine," Ursula said firmly.

Upstairs, she attacked her apartment as if it were a foe, beating the rugs, pummeling the pillows, shoving the furniture from corner to corner. There was a definite satisfaction in an old-fashioned New England spring cleaning, Ursula thought, surveying the small apartment. If only because the results were so much quicker than in a painting. The sienna-colored floor tiles were shining, windows gleamed, and the polished furniture smelled of lemon.

"So here you are," Paola said, nearly tripping over the water bucket that was holding the door of the apartment open. "I've been searching everywhere for you. What's happening here? The apartment looks beautiful but you—" She frowned. "Well—never mind."

"Thanks." Ursula laughed. "Now why don't you make yourself useful and help me move this book-case?"

Paola put down her purse and in one neat movement had pushed the bookcase back in place. "That was some quick weekend in Circeo. I don't want to say I told you so—"

"You just did," Ursula said lightly. Though she couldn't hide her disappointment from herself, she was determined not to let her friend see it.

"Well, what happened?" Paola demanded.

Ursula took her kerchief off and ran a comb through her hair. "We had dinner at a place called Mama Alfredo's, a terrific little seafood restaurant. You know, I think I've finally cultivated a taste for squid."

"Not to mention swine," Paola interrupted.

Ursula gave a rueful laugh and turned finally to meet her friend's gaze. "Okay, you were right. He was too good to be true. And like all fairy tales, it's come to an end. Finito. Now tell me—what was Professor Armado's reaction to Germany?" she said, firmly changing the subject.

That next week Ursula still avoided the Borghese Gallery, each night telling herself that she would go back to the portrait in the morning. Yet each new morning there would be something she must do

elsewhere—extra lectures to attend, a special ce-
ramics class to visit, shopping-for-Germany expedi-
tions with Paola. Determined to banish all thoughts
of Enrico, she filled time, pushing it ahead by sheer
will.

"You know, to concentrate so hard on forgetting
the count is exactly the same as remembering him,"
the canny Paola had observed, giving Ursula an
impudent grin. It was certainly going to be lonely
without her, Ursula thought, as she got ready for
their farewell evening. They were meeting at a café
and then going on to an outdoor movie held in the
ruins of the Basilica Massenzio.

It had been a while, before Circeo really, since
Ursula had taken the time to dress up. This evening
she wore the black suede trousers that showed off
her long, slim legs, and a silk shirt the same green as
her eyes. And if those eyes still refused to lighten,
remained a little too serious, too somber, well, there
was nothing she could do about that.

"Over here," Paola said, waving to Ursula from the
back of the café.

"Ciao, cara." Alberto got up, kissing her on both
cheeks.

"The ice cream here is divine," Paola said, "Alberto go get her some pistachio. Oh, how I shall
miss it—and you, little Americana, and my wicked
baby brother, who was too busy to come with us
tonight."

"The film we're going to see is a classic, I hear.
Singin' in the Rain, do you know it, Ursula?"
Alberto asked, back with the ice cream and several
friends he had collected at the bar. "Paola says Fred
Astaire is the star, but I'm sure she's wrong. It's
Gene Kelly, isn't it?"

"Actually, it's Debbie Reynolds," Ursula said, and
everyone laughed.

They were all in high spirits, arguing about films, agreeing about art, ordering brandy to pour over the ice cream. And whenever Ursula's expression became too pensive, Paola was quick to draw her back into the joviality. When Alberto finally announced that it was time for the movie, Ursula felt relieved, anxious to be part of an anonymous audience for a while, to stop forcing smiles and laughter.

Crowds were gathered in front of the Basilica Massenzio. Once a great marble building known as the Temple of Peace, the ruins were now filled with rows of chairs, spotlights, and an immense screen. Vendors carried around trays of candy and ice cream, and children, agile as little monkeys, climbed the ancient walls.

Paola clutched Alberto with one arm and Ursula with the other as they fought their way through the chaos, at last finding places very close to the screen.

The crowd already outnumbered the chairs, and tempers flared. "I've paid for myself and four children," a woman was screaming, "and now there are no seats." The police were called in, but by now others had joined in the cry. "They sell more tickets than there are seats. Arrest the management! We are not leaving!" The entire audience began to shout, a unanimous roar, until more chairs were brought in and the show finally began.

The film had been dubbed into Italian except for the songs which Ursula would hurriedly try to translate. Finally she gave up, laughing. The lightness of the story lifted her spirits, and she was surprised to find that she was really enjoying herself.

"Come on, Ursula, I'm dying of thirst," Paola said at the intermission. "Let's get something cold to drink. Alberto can watch our seats."

Holding each other's hand, they forged their way through the mob.

"Oh, no." Ursula stopped short.

"What's the matter?"

"It's Enrico," Ursula whispered in astonishment as she saw him, dressed in faded blue jeans and a bulky fisherman's sweater, pushing his way through the crowd, an ice cream cone in each hand.

"Mamma mia." Paola gave a low whistle. "It really is the Botticelli face."

Ursula restrained an impulse to turn away. Surely, she told herself, she was capable of exchanging a civil greeting.

"Does he see you?"

"I'm not sure." She gave a tentative wave, but Enrico apparently hadn't spotted her yet. How different he looked in this neighborhood crowd, dressed so informally. Even his hair seemed lighter under the basilica's spotlights, longer and curlier than she had remembered. He was coming directly toward her now. But he said nothing—he simply walked on by.

"*Asino!* Oh, that donkey!" Paola said, outraged. "The nerve—what does he think he's got to be angry about?"

But his expression hadn't even been anger, Ursula thought. She'd have preferred that to the blank look that seemed to say he no longer knew her. "Come on, let's get those Cokes," she said, trying to shrug off her hurt and bewilderment.

Yet it was not, Ursula found later that night, so easy an encounter to forget. She brewed herself two cups of chamomile tea to help her sleep, but still she lay awake, her thoughts circling around Enrico. Was it possible that he simply hadn't recognized her? But no, they'd been practically face to face. Then had he really found her rebuffal so infuriating? Was he truly that accustomed to having his way with women? Or perhaps he had pretended not to know her because he was there with one of his beautiful playmates. Yet it hadn't seemed like a pretense. His eyes had simply passed over her—like a stranger's. Oh, but the whole thing had become impossible, a bore. Disturbed, unhappy, she turned on the light and read a book about Renaissance art until finally she fell asleep.

The next morning Ursula returned to the gallery for the first time in over a week.

"Bentornato, signorina," the museum guard greeted her. "What a long time you've been away."

"Too long," Ursula said, taking her easel from him, feeling a comfort in setting it up again. The last thing Paola had said before she left was, "Finish the painting and exorcise the man." And it made sense, Ursula thought, looking at the perfect features of the young man. She could even allow herself to bask in that warm gaze—there were no consequences to suffer from a painting. She worked on the brown eyes lovingly, searching for the right lights to capture their intensity.

There were no classes that afternoon, and Ursula stayed at the gallery until it closed. Filled with the energy and the nervous high spirits that came when her work was going well, she had no inclination to go back home. Instead, she strolled through the park, wandered down the little side streets near the Piazza del Popolo, and paused to listen to a Puccini aria rising from an open window. Only when she came to a street market did she realize she had forgotten lunch. She stopped to buy a cold, wet slice of coconut and a paper cone full of roasted chestnuts, then went on, passing the fruit stalls—pyramids of rosy nectarines, purple figs, baskets of wild strawberries. A still life, Ursula thought, already planning it as she bought a huge green lime and a handful of sunny apricots.

Strolling back to Piazza del Popolo, she decided to stop at the famous Rosati's café for an iced tea. At the table next to her, some actors were discussing the good old days when Rome had been the capital of the film industry. Their voices rose, interrupting each other with the stories of their starring roles. Ursula took out her sketchbook, fascinated by one aging but still handsome man with a deeply tanned face and silver hair. Only the heavy circles under his eyes and the deep furrows on his forehead betrayed his age, just as the frayed cuffs showing beneath a well-pressed, dated suit revealed his penury. She worked quickly, noting the colors to be put in later. As she moved her chair to get a better view of the piazza in the background, she saw Enrico, and to her dismay, her heart skipped a beat. She watched him approach the café, tall and elegant in a white linen suit. Back to his usual fashionable style, she thought, and coolly, deliberately, lowered her head over her drawing.

"Well, Ursula? Aren't you going to speak to me?" he asked, stopping at her table. "Or do you wish to pretend you don't know me?"

She knew his gaze would be mocking even before she looked up to meet it. "Pretending is not *my* game," she replied.

For whatever reason he chose to ignore her barb. "Capturing the typical Roman scene? My scene, you know—I live around the corner."

It was too much, Ursula thought. An angry snub last night, today a friendly chat. And women were supposed to be capricious.

"I would like to talk to you. I wish we could have a drink now, but unfortunately"—Enrico glanced at his watch—"I have a business engagement."

"Really?" Ursula said. Liar, she thought.

"Some other time soon." He gave her a mock bow. "Arrivederci."

Ursula watched him leave, admiring his long, easy stride and wishing she had never met him. With bold, furious strokes she went back to work on her drawing.

Several days later an unexpected check from her grandmother set Ursula off on a wild shopping spree. "The momentum of work cannot be sustained indefinitely. The artist needs time to absorb, to be nurtured." Ursula repeated Professor Armado's words to herself, hoping to feel less guilty for taking the day off; worse, for enjoying it. The money could not have arrived at a more propitious moment, she thought. Just in time to buy something to wear to the gallery opening that evening. It was an important show, one she was very curious to see, and through Professor Armado had received an invitation. She'd have to remember to tell Nana Willa all that when she wrote to thank her.

The shop windows reflected springtime, were abloom with bright colors. Ursula was tempted by everything from designer jeans to a black-fringed flapper dress at a chic secondhand boutique. At very nearly the last moment, she found the perfect outfit—a creamy white satin trouser suit with a flowered cummerbund. As she dashed out of the shop, she saw Enrico leaving the bank next door. She slowed down, but he walked right past her.

"You wait," she cried, running after him, a kind of fury taking hold of her. "Wait!" She grabbed his shoulder. "Just who do you think you are, treating people like this? I've had enough of your crazy moods!"

He looked puzzled by her outburst, then gave her a tentative smile and turned as though to see if she were speaking to someone else.

"Oh, my God!" Ursula cried in disgust, and stormed away. Damn him! That perplexed, even rather sweet expression of his. What a brilliant performance—but why, for God's sake, all this acting?

The telephone was ringing when Ursula got back to her flat.

"Yes?"

"Hello, Ursula, it's me. Enrico."

Ursula said nothing. She could hardly believe it, but there was no mistaking his voice.

"Some plans of mine have changed," he was saying, "and I'm free tonight. I thought you might enjoy—"

But Ursula slammed down the receiver before he could finish. If this was the way Count Benvoglio amused himself, then the man must be quite mad. And she, Ursula promised herself, was not going to let him add any more of his craziness into her well-ordered life. Art was all she needed—all she cared about.

The Fiorella Gallery was extremely crowded when Ursula arrived. A plump woman, whose short neck was covered with ropes of pearls, gave her a program and a glass of champagne. Looking for Professor Armado, Ursula moved into a room hung with portraits and filled with furs and expensive scents.

"Darling, I thought you were in Monte Carlo with the marquis."

"What an exquisite dress, is it a Halston?"

"Principessa! Why, you look even more beautiful than your portrait."

"Good evening, Ursula." Enrico stood staring down at her.

Without a word she turned from him, pushing her way through the crowd into the refuge of a smaller room.

"Well, if it isn't my assailant. Buona sera, signorina. I hope you're not going to attack me again."

Ursula stopped, staring with unbelieving eyes at another Botticelli Man.

"May I introduce myself," he said, that full mouth turning up in a charming smile. "I am Lorenzo Benvoglio."

Five

It was like a dream, Ursula thought, a bizarre, surrealistic dream—escaping from the Botticelli Man, his classic features so distinctive in that bobbing sea of faces, only to find she had run to him and was now alone with him in this little room.

"This afternoon you spoke to me without thinking," he said, smiling broadly. "Now you think without speaking."

But, of course, it wasn't Enrico. Incredibly, unbelievably, it was his exact image. Clothes more casual, hair a little longer, it was the man of those odd encounters.

"So you two have met," Enrico said, coming into the room. His tone was cold, his face devoid of expression.

"Not what you would call officially, old man," his image said. "Won't you do the honors?"

Enrico turned to Ursula. "May I present my twin brother, Lorenzo? I have the pleasure, Lorenzo, of introducing you to Signorina Ursula Stewart." It was a begrudging, mock performance of courtliness.

"Delighted," Lorenzo said. "It is convenient to know the names of the beautiful women who attack me."

"I'm sorry," Ursula said, lowering her eyes in confusion. "I mistook you—"

Lorenzo laughed. "I know. Interesting that you should want to attack my brother, but we won't go into that now."

Ursula ignored his remark. "If you'll excuse me, I'm meeting friends," she said, and walked away, still stunned by the revelation of two Botticelli men. How detached, how impersonal Enrico's feelings for her must have been, never to have even mentioned his identical twin.

The long main room of the gallery was now overflowing with women in glittering jewels and shimmering dresses, their escorts just as elegant in perfectly tailored suits. Ursula caught a glimpse of several fellow students from the Belle Arte but still saw no sign of Professor Armado and his wife.

"Champagne, signorina?" A waiter stood before her with a tray of drinks.

"Si, grazie," she said, her words lost in the loud dialogues around her. It could have been just another cocktail party, so little attention did anybody seem to give to the paintings. And the portraits were fascinating. The artist seemed almost to be mocking his subjects—a kindly, portly gentleman, whose mouth curled slightly; a woman of great beauty, who had an uncommonly thick neck. Ursula checked the program notes again for the artist's name.

"Sergio Alessandro's a very talented portraitist, isn't he?" a man said behind her. Ursula knew without turning around that it would be Lorenzo

Benvoglio. A phrase came back from her child-hood—double trouble. No thanks, she thought, moving away to the next portrait. She had had quite enough of the Benvoglio charm.

"Don't run away again," Lorenzo said, taking her arm. "Fortunately, in this crowd you can't get far."

"Please." Ursula disengaged herself and for the first time looked directly into his eyes, dark brown eyes shaped like Enrico's but softer, warmer, without that burning intensity. "I'm not here to social-ize. I've come to see the exhibit."

"You're a serious student of art then. Good, so am I. Actually, it's my work."

"You're an artist?" Ursula asked, surprised into conversation.

"Ah, no," Lorenzo smiled. "That lucky I'm not. I work at Sotheby's in London. Director of the Im-pressionist department."

"Really?" She had never have imagined that a count could be an ordinary working man.

"Really," he affirmed, laughing at her surprise. "In fact, this is the first real holiday I've taken in two years."

Ursula gave an appropriate murmur and, deter-mined to encourage him no further, went to look at the paintings on the other side of the room.

"Now in this portrait," Lorenzo said, following her with gentle persistence, "I assure you Sergio has caught the beauty of his elegant model, Contessa Benvoglio."

"Your mother." It was not a question, so easily did Ursula recognize the familiar grace and hauteur of the elegant, dark-haired woman. "How very much you resemble her." But it was Enrico she saw in those large, dark, brooding eyes.

"Ursula!" She turned and with relief saw Profes-sor Armado calling to her from across the room.

"Now you really must excuse me," she told Lorenzo firmly, and went to join the professor and his blond, statuesque wife, who were talking to several other students from the Belle Arte.

"We've been looking for you," Professor Armado said, holding out his arm in welcome. "What a crush there is here, as they say in your country."

"No, darling, in *my* country," his young English wife, a former student, corrected.

"All right, my little chauvinist," he said fondly. "Now let's go up and see Dino's work."

It was far less crowded upstairs, far easier to study the paintings: wide-eyed, hollow-cheeked children in ghettos; a bent gray man in a gray prison cell; gaunt pregnant women with huge stomachs and sticklike arms and legs.

"Quite powerful, aren't they?" the professor said.

"Overwhelming," Ursula replied in a voice low with awe. "Downstairs the aristocracy, upstairs the masses. Odd that these two artists should have a show together."

"I'll let Dino explain that," Professor Armado said as a short, white-haired man, eating from the tray of little pizza hors d'oeuvres he carried, joined them. "This is Ursula Stewart, one of my most talented students. Dino Sabito, one of my most talented friends."

"Try one of these pizzetti," Dino said, offering the tray to Ursula. "Artists are always hungry, no?" He smiled, his teeth very white in his dark, broad-featured face. "So tell me—what do you paint?"

"Well, as I'm still studying, I suppose I do a bit of everything," she said, embarrassed by this fact. "But I'm most interested in the Renaissance period. In fact, I'm working on a reproduction of a Botticelli for this term's project."

"Oh, yes? Which?"

"A Portrait of a Youth."

"Very good. There's a great deal to be learned from the masters, artists like Botticelli and Michelangelo. They could capture the smallest line, the finest shading, and turn a blank expression into one of suffering or rapture. From them I learned how to paint eyes, to make the eyes deliver my message."

"It's a very strong one, your message."

"Ah, that's because you have a heart."

Ursula glanced back at a painting of a thin, narrow-shouldered figure in front of a faceless firing squad. "How different your work is from the portraits downstairs."

Dino laughed. "You think so? But we both paint what we see. Sergio and I have worked together for years, since I first came to Italy from Chile. First in Florence, where I made copies of the masters and he drew caricatures for a few lire. In our spare time we pursued our own art, but there was never enough spare time. So Sergio began to paint portraits of the wealthy, and they loved him. Now, whenever he has a show, I have one. And the socialites who come to see his paintings see mine. In this way," Dino said, his eyes crinkling up with his wide smile, "we help not only ourselves but the underprivileged in both our countries."

Later, when they were downstairs again, Ursula noticed a tall, thin bearded man surrounded by soignée Roman matrons and, even before Dino spoke, guessed him to be Sergio Alessandro.

"But you're too beautiful to spend your time in front of a canvas," he told her when Dino had introduced them. "You should be on it."

"Just what I was going to say." It was, to Ursula's annoyance, Lorenzo Benvoglio who spoke.

"Why, Lorenzo!" Sergio said, shaking his hand. "Your brother told me you were still in Sicily."

"Enrico is misinformed, as usual."

"And do you approve of your mother's portrait?"

"It's as charming as the contessa herself."

"Enrico has also come this evening?" Sergio inquired.

"He's over there with Stephania Pettini."

Involuntarily Ursula followed Lorenzo's gaze and, with a pang, saw Enrico in earnest conversation with a stunning black-haired young woman wearing a pale yellow, diaphanous gown—the "oil heiress" companion of the "man about town." Raising his head at that moment, Enrico seemed to return her look, or perhaps it was his twin he was casting that cold glance upon.

"Ursula!" It was Vincenzo. "How are you, bella?" He kissed her soundly on both cheeks and pulled her away to a quiet corner.

"What a long time it's been," Ursula said. "Funny—I was just thinking of Paola. I really do miss that sister of yours. What do you hear from her?"

Vincenzo laughed. "I was just going to ask you the same thing."

Absorbed in their talk of Paola and their reactions to the paintings, they stood chatting for some time.

"So here you are, Casanova," a young woman with curly red hair and a gamine smile said. "I turn my back for one moment and look what happens."

"Daniela, this is Ursula, our American friend." Vincenzo drew the young woman to him and kissed the top of her head. "You know it's true what they say about jealous redheads."

How happy he looked, Ursula thought. How happy they both looked. Ursula knew her smile was forced, the cover for an inexplicable sense of loss and momentary regret that she had not been able to fall in love with Vincenzo, that she was not the one in his embrace.

"Daniella's in medical school with me," Vincenzo said proudly.

"Really, what year?" The girl hardly looked to be eighteen.

"Like Vincenzo. My third, grazie Dio!" Daniela said. "The first two years are the most difficult."

"Nothing could be difficult for you," Vincenzo told her.

"You were," she said, smiling up at him.

Ursula stayed talking to the two lovers a few moments longer and then left them to wander the perimeter of the room, studying the paintings. Or trying to, for she was far too aware of Enrico and his glamorous companion on one side of the gallery, of Lorenzo in animated conversation with the Armados on the other. How ironic that she should be trying to avoid not one but two replicas of the very face that had captivated her heart and soul.

"I'm here to collect you, my dear," Signora Armado said, coming up to Ursula. "The party is moving on to our house. By the way, I've invited your friend along. He's quite something, that Lorenzo. He's been telling us the most amusing stories about Sotheby's."

"Has he?" Ursula said, wondering if she could plead a headache and leave. But it was already too late.

"It's all arranged," Lorenzo said, beaming, as he took each woman by the arm. "We shall lead the procession—you two, Dino and I."

As they were leaving the gallery, Enrico, looking somber, beckoned to Lorenzo.

"Pardon me a moment," Lorenzo said, going to join his twin.

It shocked Ursula to see Enrico looking so grim as they spoke, using such angry gestures, and she hurried outside, wondering what was wrong between the twins. Was this the peculiar balance of their kinship—that the stiff, arrogant brother bullied the casual, good-natured one?

"Let's go—*andiamo*," Lorenzo said cheerfully, leading the way to his car a few minutes later, as though nothing had happened.

He drove his white Alfa Romeo himself, and though it was, to be sure, an expensive and even flashy car, Ursula thought, it was without extra glitter and trimmings. And so, she had to admit, covertly watching him, was Lorenzo. There were no sophisticated airs, no aristocratic mannerisms. Though clearly he was as expert as Enrico at getting his own way, manipulative even, he did it like a happy child rather than a scheming Machiavelli.

The Armado's apartment was on the top floor of a grand seventeenth-century palazzo. Just the sort of home, Ursula thought, every artist must dream about—spacious white rooms with tall windows and immense wood beams along the high-frescoed ceilings. As for the works of art—it was like a private museum: paintings, sculpture, etchings, drawings everywhere.

In the *salotto*, casually, as well as outrageously, dressed students mixed with elegantly attired women and sophisticated-looking men. Sounds of laughter and conversation filled the room. After taking a glass of wine from a long marble-topped table, which had been set up as a bar, Ursula wandered into one of the smaller sitting rooms, where a young man was playing the piano while a woman with wild hennaed hair did a solitary exotic dance.

"A good party, isn't it?" Lorenzo said, appearing at her side. "Can I get you a drink?"

Ursula held up her wineglass. "Thanks, but I haven't even had time to start on this one."

"Then I suggest we find a quiet corner where you can give it your undivided attention. And me, of course. You're an artist, an American—that much I know but very little else. I don't even know how you met my brother."

His smile was disarming, but Ursula had no intention of sitting down to a cozy chat, least of all, a chat about Enrico. "Actually, I'm trying to find our host," she said, and before Lorenzo could protest, she went out on the terrace.

Bright paper lanterns cast wavering lights over the climbing plants and potted palms that bordered the immense sienna-colored terrace. Some guests were dancing, others flocked around a buffet of elaborate salads and ricotta pies. Making her way through the crowd, Ursula was aware of a curious ambivalence: she half-feared yet half-hoped to see Enrico. She leaned over the balustrade, looking out at the city, the domes and spires of nighttime Rome.

"Beautiful, isn't it?" Signora Armado said, beside her. "To think I was lucky enough to trade a view of Piccadilly Circus for this."

"It's fabulous. Especially from this terrace. By the way, I love the lighting effect of those lanterns. Do you think we could use them for the Masquerade Ball?"

"Did I hear Masquerade Ball? Where and when?" It was Lorenzo again.

Signora Armado smiled. "It's the Belle Arti ball. Ursula and I are in charge of the decorations."

"Perhaps I can help," Lorenzo said. "When I was in Japan, I studied origami. Astonishing how a bit of paper becomes a blooming flower, a flying bird."

"Really," Ursula said, thinking that one had at least to give him his due for originality.

"How fascinating!" Signora Armado said.

"The only thing my travels have not taught me is how to dance with two beautiful women at the same time." He looked at Ursula as he spoke. "If my hostess will do me the first honor, I'll be back to claim the next dance."

Determined to escape any more of his attentions, Ursula went back inside, where she found Professor Armado sitting hunched over a marble table, intent on a game of backgammon with Dino.

"So I owe you another million lire," he said, throwing up his hands in mock despair. "Ursula, do you know how to play?"

"It's my father's only hobby." She smiled, recalling the many excavation sites, the innumerable improvised tables on which they had played, her child's winnings proudly added up in drachmas, dinars, or rupees.

"Good," he said, getting up. "Then perhaps you'll take on the winner."

"Yes, please do." Dino half rose from his chair. "But I must tell you," he said, peering over the top of his glasses, "that I'm a crotchety old man who takes his game seriously."

But Ursula, a shrewd look coming into her green eyes, was already concentrating on her play.

They sat quietly absorbed until the end of their match. Then Dino gave a big sigh and said "Okay, I concede. The victory is yours. If you paint the way you play backgammon, then I predict great things for you."

Ursula laughed, feeling suddenly shy. "I don't thnk you can judge my work by my game."

"Bring your portfolio around to my studio sometime this week, and we'll see."

"Thank you, I'd like that."

"Have you two finished your game?"

"Ah, Lorenzo, take my place." Dino got up. "But let me warn you—she's a formidable player."

"That doesn't surprise me," Lorenzo said. "But I'm not exactly a novice myself."

He smiled and for the first time Ursula noticed a slighty chipped front tooth. She thought how much younger he seemed than Enrico.

"Well—do you accept my challenge?"

Ursula hesitated: "All right."

"Good. Loser goes out to dinner with winner," he said, reaching for her hand.

She pulled back quickly, almost as though from a flame. What was it Nana Willa always said—a burnt child dreads the fire. "I thought you were interested in the game."

"Yes, of course." Lorenzo picked up the dice.

They played slowly and carefully, professionals at the board, and Ursula won the first game. Her victory seemed to sober Lorenzo, and he took the second before her men had moved four spaces from the start.

"Well done," she said, setting up the board for the playoff.

Lorenzo moved quickly and to Ursula's consternation seemed to be winning again. She held the dice in her hands and, whispering lengthy incantations, rolled double sixes three times and promptly moved all her men off the board.

"Bravissima!" Lorenzo cried, raising his glass in a toast. "To the American champion. Now tell me—what did you say to the dice?"

"I said that it was late and time for me to go home," Ursula replied, getting up.

"Let me drive you."

"But I live only a few blocks from here. And I like the walk."

"Then let me walk with you."

"I think not," she said shortly, and then, seeing his expression, relented. To stay aloof was one thing, but to be rude was quite another. And why blame Lorenzo for his brother's faults. "Well, if you really don't mind leaving the party—"

It was after midnight, and the streets were deserted, except for the stray cats slinking into the Roman Forum to dine on the pasta the neighborhood restaurateurs had left them.

"Wouldn't you like my jacket?" Lorenzo said. "These spring nights can be very deceptive."

"But nowhere near as bad as London, I would guess."

"Oh, right. Good old foggy, rainy London. One rarely wants to walk there." He took her arm as they crossed the street, careful to release it when they reached the other side. "Bella Roma, it's good to be back."

"How much longer do you plan to stay?"

"I make it a point never to look at calendars," Lorenzo said. "It spoils holidays. Anyway, my department can survive without me if I decide to extend my holiday."

"Well, this is my street," Ursula said, as they came to little cobblestoned Via Bacino.

"I suppose you do a lot of sketching around here. You're lucky, you know, to live in this part of the city," Lorenzo said in a tone that sounded oddly wistful.

"Where do you stay when you're in the city—with your brother?"

"With Enrico? No, no. I'm staying at the Hotel Excelsior."

"Here we are—this is where I live," Ursula said, stopping in front of the huge, green, fortresslike doors that locked away her courtyard at night. "Thanks for seeing me home."

"The pleasure was entirely mine." Lorenzo bowed over her hand, raising it nearly to his lips.

That was the only moment, the only gesture, Ursula mused, climbing the steep stairs to her apartment, when he had fleetingly resembled his brother. She let herself into the flat and began slowly to undress, thinking what a strange day it had been. It seemed like weeks had passed since she had gone out shopping that afternoon. She hung up her trouser suit, pensively stroking the cool white satin, aware suddenly of a heavy weariness. Only now, alone, could she admit to her profound shock over the Benvoglio twins. What, Ursula wondered, would Paola make of so odd a development? Tomorrow she would write her about these identical twins, who were in fact so dissimilar. Paola would never believe that she now knew *two* Botticelli men. But, for that matter, did she herself?

An alley cat screeched in the night and, moving to close the shutters, Ursula drew back, startled to see a long black Mercedes parked at the corner of the tiny street. It reminded her of Enrico's. . . . But then she shook her head, as if the action could drive away memory.

Six

The next morning Ursula was awakened by the gentle harmony of church bells and the loud jovial sounds of her neighbors preparing for their Sunday picnic. She wondered if Enrico and Lorenzo spent their Sundays with the Benvoglio clan. It was easy enough to imagine Lorenzo packing the picnic hamper himself, but Enrico was hardly a likely candidate for the traditional Italian family outing. The picture, so vivid, of him with his arm around the sleek Stephania assaulted her. She rubbed her eyes vigorously, as if to obliterate the image, and chided herself for having let the Botticelli men obscure the importance of the art exhibit. Seeing Dino's work, those evocative statements of poverty, and Sergio's masterfully shrewd portraits, had been a revelation. These two men had found their way in that maze called the world of art. And here was Ursula Stewart, still a student, still confined to studying the masters. She jumped out of bed and with a purposeful stride went to the window and threw open the shutters. Today she'd get on with her own work, do some sketching at the Spanish Steps.

The Piazza di Spagna was already filled with Sunday strollers, Romans and tourists alike, when Ursula arrived there not an hour later. Passing the little Keats and Shelley Museum, she thought about the Spanish Steps of their day, when models in a rich variety of costumes had loitered about, waiting to be hired by visiting artists. Today the wide stairs steeped in a lavish display of azaleas, formed a tapestry of color against the honey-colored stone and the blue of the sky. Ursula walked up the crowded steps, through clusters of nuns, traveling youths strumming on guitars, and artists and vendors displaying their wares. As she paused to admire some bright Moroccan rugs, she noticed a beautiful barefoot boy scampering by.

"Wait," she called after him.

The child turned huge startled eyes on her, then looked away and ran faster.

"I'll get that little gypsy," the rug vendor said, darting after him.

"No, don't," Ursula cried, but he had already grabbed the frightened boy and was dragging him back.

"What did he take from you?"

"Nothing." Ursula pulled the child free. "I simply wanted to ask him to sit for me. I'm an artist." She held up her sketch pad, anxious to make her point.

The man went back to his rugs, mumbling a torrent of Arabic oaths under his breath, and Ursula gently took the boy's hand in her own.

"I didn't do anything. *Niente, niente*," he said, shaking himself free, dark curls tumbling into his round, olive-black eyes.

"Of course not. I only want to talk to you, to draw

your picture. Here." She took a thousand-lire note from her purse. "I'll pay you this if you pose for me."

The boy stared at her from beneath long, dark lashes.

"Come with me." She took his hand again, and he let her lead him over to the side of the steps, where she sat down. "Won't you sit, too?"

The child squatted beside her, watching with interest as Ursula began to sketch with bold, rough strokes. "My name is Tomaso," he offered tentatively.

"And mine is Ursula." She smiled at him. "You have a very nice face, Tomaso. I would like to paint it one day."

"If you paint me, do I get another thousand lire?"

"Yes, but you must ask your mother."

"I don't have a mother. I live with my aunt."

"How old are you, Tomaso?"

"Eight, soon I will be eight."

"Well, you're a very good model."

"Model?"

"Someone who sits still, who poses for an artist."

"Yes, I am a model," he said, his black eyes shining with pride.

"Do you spend a lot of time here?"

"Every day I'm here. I help sell jewelry with Giorgio. See him—he has on a red shirt." Tomaso pointed to a vendor at the top of the steps. "I think I better go back now."

"Okay. Take your money, you've earned it, and maybe we'll do this again."

"Oh, yes, signorina." The boy stuffed the bill into his short faded trousers. "Arrivederci, signorina."

"Arrivederci, Tomaso." Ursula watched him run up the stairs, then glanced at her sketch. It wasn't too bad for a beginning. But she wondered if she'd ever be able to capture the subtle shadows of poverty and fear that already fell across this little gypsy boy's face.

She felt a tap on her shoulder. Thinking it was Tomaso again, she turned, smiling, and found herself looking up into the gravely handsome face of Enrico.

"I saw you from the top of the steps." He hesitated. "I thought you might come and have an ice with me. We could go up to the park or to a café where it's cooler, perhaps."

His manner, friendly yet uncertain, almost took Ursula off guard. How easy it would be to fall for him again. She closed her sketchbook and stood up. "I'm sorry. I'm on my way home."

"Ursula." Enrico took hold of her shoulders gently, searching her face as he spoke. "I know you're still angry with me. I've treated you all wrong from the beginning—"

"What on earth do you mean?" Did he sit at his desk choosing various treatments for his different women, like a general plotting his strategy before battle? She shook herself free.

"Perhaps that was a poor choice of words," he said. "I'm trying to apologize. I was hoping that we could put the past behind us, that we could be friends again."

"If we had ever really been friends," Ursula said in an uncharacteristic outburst, "you might have mentioned Stephania Pettini—let alone your identical twin."

Enrico's voice and manner changed abruptly. "Lorenzo?" he said, one eyebrow rising. "What's he got to do with it? If I never mentioned him, it's because he's rarely in Rome." A frown clouded his brow. "In fact, until yesterday morning I believed him still to be in Sicily."

"Sicily?"

"Yes, that's where the family estate is." He looked away from her steady gaze. "It's a good place to relax," he said.

"I really must go now," Ursula said, and without giving him time to say anything else, she ran down the last flight of the Spanish Steps. He had simply brushed aside the reference to his oil heiress, and as for his brother, he obviously liked to give the impression that his twin did nothing more than sit around in Sicily. Did he think she wouldn't know about Lorenzo's job at Sotheby's? Was he so ashamed to have a working brother? Ursula walked faster, trying to out-distance her thoughts as last night's scenes replayed themselves: Enrico's reluctance to introduce Lorenzo, the stealthy looks he had given Lorenzo and her during the art show, the heated words when Lorenzo left the gallery. She wondered now if it hadn't, after all, been Enrico's black Mercedes parked near her apartment—spying. . . . What was Enrico's behavior all about? Ursula slackened her pace, surprised to see the sun had been obscured by a growing cluster of storm clouds. The streets were emptying as people ducked into cafés or hailed cabs, but she continued walking, relishing the now deserted streets, the light, warm rain with its sweet scent of spring.

By the time Ursula reached Via Bacino, the shower had turned into a thunderstorm, and she was thoroughly drenched, from her thin crepe summer dress to her canvas handbag. It was the latter that concerned her, for it held the sketch of Tomaso.

Once inside her flat, she took the sketch and put it on the bookcase. It had got smudged. What a pity, she thought. She would have liked to have shown it to Dino, but perhaps it would be better in any case to show him a more detailed drawing.

After getting out of her wet clothes, she wrapped herself in a corduroy robe, made a cup of tea, and curled up on the couch. Looking at the rain that fell in silvery sheets across the window pane, Ursula thought back to her room on Beacon Hill. She felt a wave of homesickness at the memory of other storms—of Nana Willa's inevitable appearance with a tray of distracting sweets, the coziness of their shared hot chocolate by the glowing fire. . . .

The prolonged, insistent ringing of the doorbell woke her.

"Signorina," the portiere was calling through the door.

The rain had stopped, and a white slip of moon lit a corner of blue-black night.

"Signorina, are you there?"

"Si, si, I'm coming." Ursula opened the door. "The storm put me to sleep—" She broke off, astonished to see Maria knee-deep in wild flowers—daisies and poppies and lilies. The hall was blooming like a country field.

"They're from the count." Beaming with excitement, Maria moved past the dazzled Ursula, bringing large baskets of wisteria and fragrant lilacs into the flat. "He came himself, can you imagine, in a little garden truck. He must be very much in love, no? You both must be, eh?" She went back into the hall, this time returning with small dainty violets and wild yellow roses. "And the count insisted on giving me ten thousand lire, can you imagine? So much money for the pleasure of bringing the flowers up to you." She put the roses in Ursula's arms. "I'm so happy for you. You were too much alone before. It's different now, eh? When he's not with you, he gives you the flowers for company."

"Take some with you, Maria. Do please," Ursula found her voice. "Here, some of these roses."

After the woman had gone, Ursula sat down on the floor among the flowers, abandoning herself to the pleasure of their scents and colors. What an astonishing, what a splendid thing for Enrico to do. Had she been too critical, too harsh in her judgment of him? The telephone rang, interrupting her thoughts.

"Ursula—have you received my little nosegay?" The voice was not Enrico's. "Tell me, are they your favorites, at least some of them?"

"Lorenzo?" Ursula ignored the strange sense of disappointment she felt. "They're beautiful. I don't know how to thank you."

"I do—have dinner with me."

"No, I'm sorry." Her glance fell on the forgotten sketch of Tomaso. "I've work to do. But thanks again, Lorenzo. I've never seen so many beautiful flowers."

For a moment Ursula sat quite still, smiling wryly as she looked at the overflowing baskets around her. Maria, of course, had no idea there were two counts, but Ursula, who did, had instantly assumed the flowers were from Enrico. Why? Enrico's gesture would have been a sophisticated Peruvian orchid from Rome's most exclusive florist. This warm, spontaneous offering could only have been his twin's. She smiled as she thought of Lorenzo gathering wild flowers. How impulsive he was, and, yes, sensitive, too. And yet her first thought had been of Enrico. Perhaps if she had met Lorenzo first, if he had been the Botticelli Man.... Ursula got up, shaking her head, as though to free herself of any further fancies. No, she refused to be encumbered any longer with thoughts of either of the counts Benvoglio. She took the sketch of Tomaso to her drawing board and set to work, enthusiasm for the little gypsy boy quickly banishing any lingering thoughts of her dilemma.

Though Rome had the reputation of being an international capital, its character was that of a small village; one was always running into friends, glimpsing the same faces until they, too, became friends. Determination alone was not enough, Ursula found, to keep the Benvoglio men out of her life. She would find herself tense and on guard whenever she was in the neighbourhood of Piazza di Spagna, afraid of another encounter with Enrico. As for Lorenzo, he continued his casual but persistent suit, calling to suggest an afternoon at the horse races, a supper picnic at Lake Bracciano. And when she pleaded work or a previous engagement, he would, with good humor, keep her on the phone chatting in his warm and easy way.

One afternoon Lorenzo telephoned to ask her to the opening of The Orange, a trendy new discotheque. He was, he said, sending over a proper invitation in the form of three bushels of oranges. When Ursula protested this extravagance, he laughed.

"But I picked these oranges myself. I brought them back with me from Sicily."

Not wanting to mention her encounter with Enrico, or that he had told her that Lorenzo had been in Sicily, Ursula said, "Sicily? But I thought you were in London."

"To be sure I was in London. But I always start my holidays in sunny Sicilia. Is this so surprising?"

"Not at all," Ursula said quickly. "It's just that you didn't mention it before."

Lorenzo laughed. "Had I known you were so interested, I most certainly would have told you sooner. But perhaps I can tell you more about Sicily another time—tomorrow night at dinner?"

"I'm afraid I can't."

"Wednesday? Thursday? Venerdi? Sabato?"

Ursula's sigh fell between amusement and annoyance. "Look, Lorenzo, this is a very busy week. I've got to work on my term project, and there's the Masquerade Ball this weekend, which means I'm going to be up to my neck in paper flowers."

"And what else? Have you chosen your costume yet?"

"That," Ursula replied, "just may turn out to be the best-guarded secret in Rome."

"I like a challenge," Lorenzo said and, laughing, hung up.

In the following days, so hectic with lectures, workshops, and committee meetings, Ursula still managed her mornings at the gallery. But far from giving her the kind of solace it used to, the *Portrait of a Youth* only increased her confusion about the Benvoglio twins. She doubted that she had any objectivity left; it seemed almost as though her subconscious held the brush. One day she would find herself painting Enrico's mocking expression, the next, a mole that belonged to Lorenzo. Time, she consoled herself, would change it all. And for a little while she managed to believe this.

"One more lantern should do it. An orange one," Signora Armado said, looking more like a fellow

The Botticelli Man

student in her blue jeans and work shirt than a faculty wife. "What do you think?"

Ursula glanced around the Belle Arti's huge assembly room. Garlands of paper flowers blossomed in midair, great bouquets hung down from the ceiling like rainbow-colored chandeliers. A banquet table gleamed with silver at one end of the room, at the other an ornate platform trimmed in fluted gold paper awaited the band. "I would say that completes the disguise beautifully—academia is masked for the ball."

"But we are not," Signora Armado said. "Do you know what time it is? We've left ourselves hardly an hour to get ready. It's going to take me that long just to put on Empress Josephine's headdress. How clever you were to bring your costume with you."

"Oh, it wasn't cleverness." Ursula laughed. "I just made the mistake of agreeing to take over Paola's job on the food committee. I knew the caterers would never get here on time."

"When in Rome," Signora Armado said vaguely. She blew a friendly kiss and hurried away, nearly colliding at the door with a parade of white-jacketed waiters arriving in a confusion of parcels and trays and frenzied exclamations.

"Signorina, where do you want the drinks?"

"Mamma mia, we forgot the ice!"

"Signorina, there were no rice balls so we brought pomodori al risotto," a small fat man said, flourishing a tray of roasted tomatoes bursting with rice, garlic, and bits of potato.

It wasn't until after the musicians and some early masqueraders had arrived that Ursula was finally able to dash into Professor Armado's classroom to transform herself from a harried worker into a cool Renaissance lady. From a long white box she took the costume she and Paola had spent so many evenings sewing; a lilac dress bordered in purple velvet, with a close-fitting bodice and low neckline. She pulled it carefully over her head, sliding her arms into the long, narrow sleeves that ended in points at the back of her hands, and fastened a golden girdle low over her hips. Brushing back the long purple velvet tippets that flowed to the ground from her shoulders, she put a gold chain band around her head and hurried back down to the ball.

Breathless and suddenly a little shy, Ursula stood at the entrance, watching elegant pompadoured ladies, armed buccaneers, a luminously sad Pierrot. She waved to Professor Armado, barely disguised as Napoleon, and then stood transfixed, staring at a vision on the other side of the room. It was the *Portrait of a Youth.* No modern-day version, but the real Renaissance man, who now left his doorway frame and walked toward her. He wore a short, blue-velvet, quilted tunic with elaborate brass hooks and an ornamental love knot tied around his neck. Black hose covered his long, straight limbs, and a golden girdle holding a dagger was belted at his narrow hips. His dark hair was parted at the side and fell in soft curls around his pale, serious Botticelli face.

"May I have the honor of this dance?" he asked, suddenly breaking into a smile.

Ursula blinked. It was Lorenzo standing before her.

"A Renaissance woman really shouldn't be without her Renaissance man. Especially in this dangerous place. Look—Dracula is over there. And Machiavelli only a few steps away, with Cesare Borgia, no doubt."

Ursula laughed. "You win," she said, and followed Lorenzo onto the dance floor. He was charming and delightful, and she could no longer resist him. And indeed, she thought, why should she? Why should she refuse to go out with him just because of his twin? And now that the work for the ball was finished, she would have more time. Still, as Lorenzo took her in his arms, she couldn't help wishing that it was Enrico she was dancing with. . . .

Seven

Standing outside Dino Sabito's door, portfolio in hand, Ursula was suddenly filled with doubts. What if it had been no more than social small talk that had prompted his offer to look at her work? She pressed the bell but heard no ring, so she knocked firmly. What she had brought was for the most part standard—nudes, a few landscapes and still lifes, some watercolors of Rome. She had hesitated long over her *Portrait of a Youth* and in the end had left it behind, feeling it still too incomplete. It was the study of Tomaso that had given her the courage to make this appointment with Dino. She had re-worked the preliminary sketch of the little gypsy boy into a series that could be the basis for an oil painting. Unless, of course, she was deluding herself. Well, she'd find that out soon enough—someone was opening the door.

"Ursula, how punctual you are." Dino, looking smaller in his serapelike smock, a streak of green paint in his frizzy white hair, took her hand. "Please come in. You will excuse the mess. I don't seem to be able to work when things are too orderly." He led the way through a dark vestibule into a sun-filled studio. Three easels were placed at different angles beneath the large skylight, the works in progress carefully covered. Canvases were stacked along the walls, and the floor was littered with abandoned sketches.

"I've got two folding chairs somewhere," Dino said, looking under a long table cluttered with paints, palettes, sketchbooks, and Spanish newspapers. "Well, perhaps we'd do better in the kitchen. There I know are chairs. And coffee."

Ursula nodded, too nervous by now for ordinary conversation.

The kitchen, however, was no more than an extension of the studio. Two marmalade-colored cats slept among discarded tubes of paint near an open window. In the sink were cups filled with brushes, and the round wooden table was piled high with art books and journals.

"You know you've nothing to be nervous about," Dino said, motioning Ursula to a chair, then gently taking the portfolio from her. "We're just two artists exchanging ideas. Perhaps you would be kind enough to make the coffee while I look at your work."

"Oh, yes." Ursula, grateful to have a task, jumped up from her chair so quickly that one of the cats roused himself to give her an irritated snarl.

Never had time moved so slowly, if indeed it moved at all, while Dino, his thick brows knitted in concentration, studied her drawings. He returned to the sketches of Tomaso again and again, his coffee untouched, and by now, Ursula was sure, quite cold.

"Well?" she said, unable to sustain the silence any longer.

Dino smiled at her and nodded. He picked up his espresso, drank it in one swallow, looked down at the gypsy boy again, and finally spoke. "There's no question you have talent, Ursula. What you choose to do with it—ah, that's something else." He gave her a speculative but kind look. "It's no easy thing the life of an artist. It is an—obsession. Hard work whose reward is only the knowledge that you have not yet worked quite hard enough."

"I'm beginning to realize that."

"So then let's get down to specifics. I think you tend to be, understandably, a little too academic. There's too much control. But with time you will relax and learn to trust yourself. Already I see it with the boy, it's very interesting what you've caught. If I were you, I should try a portrait of this child."

"That's just what I want to do," Ursula said, excitement and pleasure at last breaking through her embarrassed reserve. "But you know, I'm not sure I can really translate what I see in Tomaso to canvas."

Dino smiled. "If you *were* sure, you would not, I think, be an artist. If it will make you feel secure, come and paint here. You can clear out a corner of the studio for yourself. Sometimes it helps to have a comrade in work."

These last words Ursula treasured perhaps most of all, repeating them over to herself as she walked to the Piazza di Spagna to look for Tomaso. She had hoped for encouragement, yes, but to have an artist like Dino Sabito call her a comrade, be willing to help her—that really was luck. And the joy of being able to tell her father, not write him the news but actually tell him. She felt in her pocket for the cable that had come that morning announcing his unexpected arrival.

It was nearly two o'clock by the time Ursula got to the Spanish Steps. Most of the vendors were still there, sitting next to their displays and eating pasta and drinking wine, but neither the little gypsy boy nor the jeweler he worked for were among them. Obviously they had gone home for the siesta. She considered doing the same but then decided in favor of going to Babington's to celebrate her good fortune.

Babington's, an English-style tearoom, was a venerable institution of the Piazza di Spagna, a favorite rendezvous for artists since the nineteenth century. Now film stars and poets and old titled ladies with young untitled men came to eat Welsh rarebit at its small mahogany tables. Even on a spring afternoon such as this, there would be a fire blazing in the red brick hearth, while sedate black-aproned waitresses served tea and hot scones. It was cozy and restful, a place to sort out thoughts.

Ursula pushed the door open just as someone was coming out, and staggering backward, she dropped her portfolio, which came untied. Drawings were scattered on the floor.

"My dear, I'm so sorry—are you quite all right?" a woman inquired, her English accent so perfect and refined it could only belong to an Italian.

"Yes," Ursula said, glancing anxiously at her work.

"Enrico, don't just stand there. Help the poor girl pick up her things."

Ursula froze at the sound of the name and slowly looking up, saw Enrico and the handsome Countess Benvoglio of Sergio's portrait.

"Allow me, signorina." Enrico moved stiffly

toward Ursula and, his face utterly composed, un-smiling, quickly gathered up the drawings. "I hope you are not hurt," he said, averting his eyes as he handed her back the portfolio.

Not trusting herself to speak, Ursula shook her head, quickly tied the portfolio closed, then rushed into the tearoom. Signorina, indeed. The nerve of him, pretending not to know her. Clearly he hadn't wanted to introduce her to his mother. Well, a foreigner in a rather shabby denim skirt, carrying a portfolio, was hardly material to present to the countess. Ursula was almost amused by such anti-quated snobbery. She had been publicly "cut"—yes, that was Nana Willa's term for it. But despite the amusement, her cheeks continued to burn as she went to a small table in the back of Babington's.

Thank heavens, Ursula thought, that Lorenzo didn't share his family's loftiness. She wondered if Enrico knew they had been going out together, perhaps this, too, explained the snub, for since the Masquerade Ball she had seen him several times. She poured herself a cup of tea from the silver pot the waitress had brought, watching the deep amber cloud with milk, her thoughts settling on Lorenzo. Though she meant to let their friendship develop slowly, it was not always easy to resist his impetu-ousity and his spontaneity. Yet for all his determi-nation to be in her company, there was nothing of the seducer in his manner. Unlike Enrico, Lorenzo treated her with almost old-fashioned gallantry and respect. She also admired Lorenzo's sense of adven-ture. He had told her about a safari he had been on in Africa, a trip to the Arctic, and other travels. Yet he still managed to hold an important job at Sotheby's, where, as he put it, he could live the greatest adventure of all—Art.

Ursula finished her scones and poured out the

last of the tea, smiling as she recalled Lorenzo's boyish insistence on making a mystery of their date this evening. She must dress up, he had said, for he was taking her to a "surprise." Well, she would have a few surprises for him, too. She took out the crumpled telegram from her father and, smiling, read once again: EN ROUTE LONDON. STOPOVER ROME. WILL CALL ON ARRIVAL. ALL LOVE PAPA.

That evening, sitting in the low bucket seat of Lorenzo's small, mud-spattered Alfa Romeo, Ursula looked like a misplaced queen. A delicately wrought tiara of emeralds, which had belonged to her mother, crowned Ursula's blond head, matching the green silk dress so elegantly draped over her tall, slender frame. As they drove through the city traffic, she told Lorenzo about her father's cable and her visit with Dino. He complimented her on the latter but was far more interested to hear about Professor Stewart.

"And is his trip to London because of some exciting new archaeological discovery?" he asked.

"Yes, I suppose so, but I won't say another word until you tell me where you're taking me."

"I'll only tell you that it's outside of Rome. And another clue—you'll be able to do something you're very good at."

"Paint?" Ursula asked, puzzled.

"You'll see." Lorenzo laughed and stepped on the gas. "You know I'm very anxious to meet your father. I will have the opportunity, won't I?"

"Yes," she said, and wondered if her father would conside this an intrusion on his brief visit. She had to admit that she herself felt a little that way; still, they could spend the afternoon together, and then perhaps Lorenzo could join them for dinner.

"How long has your father been in Egypt? Does he teach at the University in Cairo, or is he involved only with the dig?"

Ursula, touched by his interest, spoke long and easily of her father, warming, as always, to the subject. He listened carefully as he drove, every now and then interrupting to ask for a specific detail of her father's work.

"I don't want him to think I'm an ignorant upstart."

"Why, Papa would never think that," Ursula said. "How could he, with all you've done and your position at Sotheby's. By the way, one of his dearest friends works there—Mr. Hamilton—do you know him?"

"What does he do?"

"He works with old manuscripts, costumes—that sort of thing."

"Quite a different department," Lorenzo said. He signaled a turn. "We're nearly there."

Ursula could sense the excitement behind his smile and, glancing out the window, saw that the narrow road was curving through a familiar park. "I think I've been here before. Yes, that villa, I know it." She spoke more to herself, her mind racing back to the evening she and Enrico had stopped here on the way to Circeo. The old villa looked different now: bright lights shone from every window, and there was the faint sound of music.

"You've been here before? But when? With whom?"

"Enrico stopped here on the way to Circeo—" Ursula blushed but made herself meet Lorenzo's eyes. She had never mentioned that abortive visit to Circeo, but she could see from his expression that he knew.

"And why was he stopping here?"

"He said he had some business to take care of. I didn't go inside with him, he wanted me to wait in the car." Remembering that night, she couldn't quite keep the bitterness from her voice, and she tried to cover it with a laugh. "I went for a walk and met a crazy old lady who seemed to think Enrico was a notorious gambler."

Lorenzo sighed, then said quietly, "She wasn't crazy, Ursula."

Ursula stared at him in the dimness of the car. "Are you teling me it's true, that Enrico's a gambler?"

"Oh, there's nothing wrong with gambling. I brought you here tonight so we could play. But my brother tends to get carried away—he's what they call compulsive."

Ursula hardly knew what to say. Whatever faults Enrico had, it was still somehow difficult to see him in this role of the obsessed gambler. "It must be hard for your parents."

"Yes, it is—but we came here to enjoy ourselves, not to discuss Enrico." As he helped Ursula out of the car, he gave her a gay smile. "Come and be my lady luck."

"Do you know I've never been to a casino before?"

Lorenzo laughed. "Ironic that I should be the twin who corrupts you," he said, ringing the great brass bell.

A tall, stout man, his bulky body threatening to burst through the seams of his tuxedo, opened the door. "What's the name?" he asked in a deep, gruff voice.

Ursula recoiled, horrified at the long scar on his right cheek. He looked like a thug out of an old gangster movie, totally at odds in this exquisite setting of gold velvet, of marble staircases, and high, sculptured ceilings.

"Count Lorenzo Benvoglio and Signorina Stewart," Lorenzo said.

"Wait."

"A rather unsavory-looking character, isn't he?" Ursula said, as the man walked heavily up the stairs.

"He's what is generally known as a bouncer." Lorenzo laughed at Ursula's expression. "Don't look so surprised. You've no idea how much money circulates through this place. Somebody has to be tough enough to keep out the undesirables."

The bouncer returned, accompanied by a very distinguished, white-haired gentleman.

"Signore Rosa," Lorenzo said. "How nice to see you. May I present Signorina Stewart?"

Signore Rosa bowed low over Ursula's hand, then turned a stern face to Lorenzo. "I must tell you that Count Enrico has been here—"

"Yes, yes, I know," Lorenzo interrupted, drawing him to a corner of the foyer, where the conversation continued in urgent whispers.

"I tell you I cannot!" Signore Rosa said, shaking his head. "It can't be got around this time."

Lorenzo's excited reply, whatever it was, was punctuated with wild gestures.

"Do I have your word?" Signore Rosa asked. "No, it's better that I have your signature." He bowed in Ursula's direction and left.

"Damn that brother of mine," Lorenzo said. "He certainly got himself into trouble this time."

"Surely they don't expect you to be your brother's keeper," Ursula protested.

"Better me than my parents." Lorenzo led her into the main room, where tuxedoed gentlemen gathered around the different game tables. "But please, let's forget it. We're here to enjoy ourselves, remember?"

The Botticelli Man

Of the handful of ladies who were present, several were beautiful and very young, while the others, dressed in black, looked like ancient crows, as they perched on their high stools. Voices were hushed, the loudest sounds coming from the spinning of the ball in the roulette wheel, the shuffling of cards, the "rien ne vas plus" of the croupiers. Smiling with surprise, Ursula noted the painted ceiling—naked, voluptuous women puffing at cigarettes and cigars, only their feet modestly covered. Who would have thought that the decadent art of the late nineteenth century would decorate this great Renaissance relic.

"Wait here a minute, darling, will you, while I go buy some chips," Lorenzo said, leaving Ursula at the small bar in the corner of the room.

"I must say I'm surprised to see you here again."

Startled, Ursula realized this remark was addressed to herself and came from the old dowager she had met on her other visit.

The woman studied her. "Are those real emeralds?" she asked, pointing to the tiara.

Even more startled by this, Ursula managed a cool smile, unwilling to confide that it was her most prized possession, left to her by the mother she had never known. "It's only a trinket, signora."

"If you're here with the count again, be careful that he doesn't gamble your trinket away."

"You should be certain of whom you are speaking before you slander them," Ursula replied, feeling her cheeks grow hot.

"I know of whom I am speaking, my dear. It seems a pity that you do not." And giving a shrill laugh, the woman walked away.

"A friend of yours?" Lorenzo asked, returning just then, his pockets bulging with chips.

"Hardly. That's the lady I told you I met in the park when I was here before. She thinks I'm with the gambler again."

"Well, most people, as you know, cannot tell us apart. But come, there's a table here set up just for you."

"But I've never played any casino games."

"Oh, yes, you have." Taking her arm, Lorenzo escorted Ursula to a backgammon table. "Remember?"

"But that was just for fun."

"With money it's also for fun—only more so. Here are some chips."

"But that's your money," Ursula protested.

"Don't be silly." He put a handful of chips in her bag. "While you're winning at this table, I shall retire to the inner sanctum for a more serious game. Each chip is worth twenty thousand lire, so play wisely. Show me what a champion you really are!"

"You're going to leave me?" She couldn't keep the disappointment out of her voice.

"Only for a little while. I'm not allowed to take you into the private game."

Watching Lorenzo cross the room and disappear through a tall, ornate door, Ursula felt peculiarly abandoned, out of place among these people so intent upon their games, so unapproachable. Even the croupiers repeating the same words, the same gestures, were as aloof and unreal as wind-up dolls.

"Place your bet, signorina."

Ursula hesitantly took a chip from her bag and pushed it toward the dark, sleek young man on the other side of the table.

"There's a twenty-five thousand lire minimum."

"Oh, dear." She fumbled in her bag. "I've no change. I only have twenty-thousand-lire chips."

"I'll give you change," the croupier said, not bothering to hide his disdain.

"Don't bother. I'll bet the forty thousand."

The young man's still composure began to crumble as they played and he saw Ursula was not the naive beginner he had assumed. She rolled the dice, her eyes flashing with excitement. Already she had a good lead over him. Just one pair of high doubles and the game would be hers. She shook the dice for a long moment and then, holding her breath, threw.

"Double fives."

Ursula could hardly believe it as the croupier returned her money threefold.

"Again?" he asked, setting up the board and looking at her with something like admiration.

"Why not?" She put down sixty thousand lire this time. If she lost she'd still have far more than Lorenzo had given her.

For a while, in the excitement of her winning streak, Ursula lost track of time. But by the end of her fourth game, she began to wonder what had become of Lorenzo.

"You're very lucky tonight," the dealer said, eyeing the mountain of chips beside Ursula.

"Yes, I guess I am. Tell me," she said, neatly stacking her winnings, "what do they play in that private room?"

"Poker. I daresay you have enough there to join the game."

"Oh, no." Ursula laughed, shaking her head. "I think I'll quit while I'm ahead."

"My, my! Complimenti!" Lorenzo said, coming up behind her. "It looks like you broke the bank. I knew you could do it."

"Oh, good, you're back." Ursula said happily. "Let's go have a drink—my treat."

"Fine. But first I'll just take a few of these to finish my game." Lorenzo filled his pockets with Ursula's winnings. "I'll meet you at the bar." He was gone again before Ursula could reply, and slowly she made her way to the bar. How blithely he had taken all the chips and left her alone again. It was his money, of course. But it would have been so much more fun if they had gambled together, even lost it all. She kept her eyes on the door through which Lorenzo had vanished, willing him to come out, to quell the doubts that were growing in her mind. Was he so different from Enrico after all?

"Here I am, darling," Lorenzo said, reappearing at last. "Now, shall we try our luck at roulette, or do you prefer blackjack?"

"It's getting awfully late. And my father arrives tomorrow morning, you know."

"But, of course. Come, I'll take you home."

Lorenzo was particularly attentive on the ride back to Rome, as though apologizing for having neglected her for so much of the night.

"How lovely you are," he said, as they sat parked in front of her building. "My lovely, lucky girl." He took her in his arms and kissed her. "Buona notte," he whispered, "buona notte, carissima."

Later, Ursula lay awake wondering about that kiss. How ordinary, commonplace a kiss it had seemed. Why? And why must she still remember Enrico's touch? Her reason told her she was much better off with Lorenzo. Did sense and sensuality, she asked herself, have to be as different as pleasure and pain?

"Hello, my dear. I'm here," Professor Stewart announced over the telephone, his voice sounding very far away.

The Botticelli Man

"In Rome?" Ursula asked. "Are you calling from the hotel?"

"No, I'm at the airport. I've got to arrange for a seat on the midnight flight to London, and then I'll grab a cab and be right with you."

"Hurry, hurry!" Ursula cried into the phone. It was useless to complain that he wasn't staying any longer. Perhaps on the way back he would.

She tidied the room, rearranging the bust of her father on the bookshelf. It had turned out rather well, and as soon as she had the money, she would get it bronzed for Nana Willa. She put out a bottle of wine to have with lunch and then stood at the window watching for her father's taxi. It seemed to be taking hours, but she did not leave her vigil, so anxious was she for that first glimpse of him.

"Papa, Papa!" Ursula shouted down like any of her Italian neighbors when finally Professor Stewart arrived. She raced out of the apartment, down the stairs, and into his arms. "I've missed you so much." She hugged him, feeling like a little girl. "I hadn't even realized how much until now."

"Me, too, sweetheart. It feels like it's been years, not months."

Maria came out to greet the professor, as did her grandson and the woman who owned the bakery across the street.

"Now, let me look at you," Ursula said, when finally she had got her father upstairs. Perhaps he was tired and a bit thinner, but he looked well. His eyes, the same clear green as her own, were shining bright. His wild gray hair was even longer than usual, making him look like a mad professor. "You look fine—a little too thin, maybe."

"Now, Ursula, why don't we leave such observations for your grandmother? Anyway, it's I who am supposed to be doing the inspecting."

"And what do you think?" Ursula asked, twirling around.

"Beautiful, as always. I might even say more beautiful."

"Still the charmer, I see. Come sit down and have some lunch. I still don't even know why you're going to London. Not that it matters, as long as I get to see you."

"A jug of Chianti, mozzarella, and tomatoes." Professor Stewart beamed. "A nice change from cous-cous, believe me."

Ursula filled her father's glass and cut the loaf of crisp brown bread. "*Benvenuto,*" she said, sitting down across from him. "Now, tell me what you found."

"All right—class begins. We discovered some limestone statues, and that, of course, is the reason for London. I've never seen anything like them. They could be from the Ramesside Period. Hard to say since there was an attempt to return to the classic art of the earlier New Kingdom at that time. So now you're as well informed as your old man. But, dear girl, it's you I want to talk about. How's the work going? Not a bad likeness that," he said, nodding in embarrassed approval at his bust. "Tell me, how's the Botticelli portrait getting on?"

"Slow. I'm about to start a new portrait, though." She ran to get her portfolio and showed him the sketches of Tomaso as she recounted her visit with Dino.

"But this is marvelous," Professor Stewart said, his face reflecting her own pride and pleasure. "Yes, yes, your style is changing, maturing," he murmured studying the little gypsy boy intently. "These are full of promise, full of promise. Now let me see the rest of the portfolio."

His bright, intelligent eyes examined each piece

of work carefully. When he came to the Botticelli Man, he broke his silence. "My God, Ursula, this is remarkable. There's such life, so much vitality here. It's as though you had a live model."

"Well, I do know someone who looks incredibly like the original youth," Ursula said, thinking of Enrico.

"You're not serious," Professor Stewart began, but broke off as he saw her expression.

"Papa, I wonder if you'd mind very much if a friend of mine joined us for dinner? He's so anxious to meet you."

"I'd be happy to meet him, my dear. Is he somebody at the school?"

Ursula smiled. "No, he's Count Lorenzo Benvoglio. He's here on holiday. He works in London at Sotheby's—head of the Impressionist department."

"I see. And I gather he has something to do with the authenticity of the Botticelli portrait?"

"Yes and no," Ursula said, blushing furiously. She was tempted to tell her father about Enrico—and yet why bother, when it was Lorenzo he was going to meet.

That evening Lorenzo took Ursula and Professor Stewart to Guilio's, a restaurant that, he assured them, they would thoroughly enjoy. It was hidden away in a little cul-de-sac near the Roman Forum. The cellar dining room with its crumbling terracotta walls and ancient stone pillars greatly appealed to Professor Stewart, as did his first taste of fried zucchini flower stuffed with mozzarella and anchovies.

"Delicious," he said, "an absolutely Lucullan banquet."

Ursula leaned back and sipped her wine. She

sensed that her father was holding himself a little aloof from Lorenzo's friendly charm. Still, she told herself, that was often his way, and, even so, the evening seemed to be a success.

"Ursula tells me you're with Sotheby's," Professor Stewart said. "You must know Matthew Hamilton— he's a great friend of mine."

Lorenzo glanced up from his salad. "No, I'm afraid I rarely leave my Impressionists."

"That reminds me. There were some Bonnards in your last catalog. I'll have to stop by when I'm in London, just for the pleasure of a close look."

"Oh, all the Bonnards were sold at the auction, instantly."

"Really?" Professor Stewart looked startled. "I thought that some were being withheld until a family dispute was settled. But perhaps I'm wrong."

Lorenzo paused, narrowing his eyes thoughtfully. "No, no, you're quite right," he said finally. "Silly of me to have forgotten. I'm afraid this delicious wine has made me rather slow. Yes, we're being plagued with lawyers and screaming heirs. It's a relief to be in Rome."

"I can imagine," Professor Stewart said quietly.

Eight

A heavy dampness pervaded the empty classroom where Ursula sat alone staring out the window at the rain and intermittent sunshine. The green courtyard looked dim, the bright flowers blurred. She looked up at the sky, thinking it was as full of uncertainty as her heart. Lorenzo had invited her to Circeo to meet his parents. "It is time," he had announced. Some trick of her imagination had made him speak in Enrico's smooth, deep tones, and her heart had started to pound. Why didn't Lorenzo himself set off these same inexplicable emotions? Still, he was kind and reliable, and surely that was better than excitement.

"Ursula, is that you?" Professor Armado said, coming into the room and turning on the light.

"I got here a bit early."

"So I see." He shook out his coat and umbrella. "Dino tells me you've cleaned out a spot for yourself at his studio. Good for you, I shouldn't have thought it possible. He's quite impressed with your work, you know."

"Thanks. He's been awfully kind. And so have you, professor."

"Bosh, as my wife says. Ah, here comes the rest of my class. As a handful of wet, bedraggled students wandered into the room, Professor Armado said, "Take your seats everybody." He waited until they had sat down, then said, "We will begin with a discussion of Michelangelo's work. You are all familiar with *The Creation of Adam*, are you not?"

The class's silence was interpreted as an affirmation.

"Michelangelo," the professor continued, passing a print around the room, "portrayed God in human form but preserved the idea of a transcendent power behind the universe. The essence of the creation is contained in the gesture of the hands. Would you explain why, Signorina Stewart?"

Ursula turned from the window to the teasing gleam in Professor Armado's eye. He thought he'd caught her daydreaming, did he? "The gesture of the hands shows the life-force that is being communicated to a rather listless, inert Adam."

"Brava," Professor Armado said. "So we see the essence of creation idealized in body and in mind . . ."

Ursula continued her train of thought. How strange it would be to go to Circeo again, this time really to meet the count and countess. Remembering her encounter with Enrico and his mother at Babington's, she winced. Surely the countess would remember it, too? Well, if the weekend turned out to be another fiasco, it might be for the best. It would be a relief to be the mistress of her heart again. The Benvoglio twins had become too much the center of her life, consuming her time and thoughts. It was almost as if Paola's oft-repeated jest had come true. "One day you're going to wake up and find yourself in Renaissance Italy with your Botticelli Man, and you'll spend the rest of your days pining for the 1980's." Amused by the recollection of the loving, acerbic Paola, Ursula began to plan her wardrobe for the weekend. She would have to remember to pack her riding boots, as well as a bathing suit, for surely it would be warm enough to swim.

Yet the next afternoon, driving along the familar rocky seacoast, Ursula was again filled with apprehension. The countess had appeared to be so haughty, formidable really. Would the old count be any less so? How could she, an American art student, possibly fulfill their expectations for Lorenzo? Would Miss Peabody's etiquette do for the Roman aristocracy?

"You're awfully quiet," Lorenzo said, gazing at her with concern. "Aren't you pleased to be going to Circeo?"

"Just a little nervous." Ursula smiled. "I'm not exactly used to weekending in the country with nobility."

Lorenzo shrugged. "Not to worry."

"You've never really told me what your parents are like."

"No? Well, let's see. My father is a tall chap with a little white beard. To his friends he is 'Dottore.' Of course he's not a doctor of medicine, but I suppose he is one of history. He's writing a biography of his ancestor, Enrico Benvoglio—a great friend of Vasari's."

"Really? Why didn't you tell me this before?"

"I didn't think you'd be interested."

"Lorenzo, how can you say that?" Ursula said,

staring at him. "You know the Renaissance is my period. I'm always anxious to learn more about it. There are so many unanswered questions, unidentified paintings."

He patted her hand. "But of course. Perhaps you'll be able to discuss it with him."

They drove in silence for a few moments and then, "What about your mother?" Ursula asked.

"Ah, her." Lorenzo paused, his face clouding over. "She's beautiful, busy, and, quite often, I fear, a bitch."

"Lorenzo, you don't mean that!"

"Oh, I do mean it, sweet girl. I love her, but she has always been so occupied dealing with my twin that she has very little time for anyone else."

"Oh, but, Lorenzo—"

"Believe me, I know what I'm talking about. But look, we're almost there," Lorenzo said happily, just as Enrico had, as they drove through the high gray stone gates and into the orange grove. This time Ursula could see the tall, green, leafy trees with their plump, bright fruit.

"Open your window and take a deep breath."

It was eerie the way he was repeating everything Enrico had said. Ursula felt chilled. Was this some sort of omen? A warning, perhaps? Oh, stop this nonsense, she scolded herself, it's too childish.

They drove up to the villa, a splendid sight, bright white against the blue of the sky. "Signore Lorenzo, how good to see you," cried old Pina, rushing out to meet the car. "I'm so glad you've finally come. And a signorina, too!" She turned startled eyes on Ursula. "But it is the same signorina who was here before. What a surprise."

Ursula cringed as if struck, but Lorenzo smoothed over the awkward moment with charm.

"Yes, Pina, but it would be better if you said nothing to Mama and Papa about the signorina's last visit. You understand?" he said, putting his arm around the old nurse.

"My lips are sealed," Pina assured him, giving Ursula a toothless grin.

"Where is everyone?" Lorenzo asked, as they followed her into the house.

"The contessa is napping, the conte is working, and the signorino has gone down to the sea to bathe."

Signorino? A young cousin from Sicily, perhaps, Ursula thought. It might be easier with another guest.

"Good. Then we'll have time to freshen up before we see everyone for cocktails," Lorenzo told Ursula. "Come, I'll show you to your room."

"Really—it's such a beautiful villa," Ursula murmured nervously, trying to quell the memory of the last time she had climbed the red-carpeted staircase.

Lorenzo led her down the long hallway and into a large room with windows that opened onto a balcony. White ruffles covered the four-poster bed and delicate vanity table, and the soft breeze blowing through pale yellow curtains carried the scent of the sea.

"It's perfect—I love it," Ursula said, relieved at how different it was from the silky, seductive boudoir Enrico had chosen for her. She stepped out onto the little terrace. "Oh, what a heavenly view."

"That path goes through the garden down to the sea. Can you smell it?"

Ursula nodded, already intoxicated by the salt air.

"Well, I'll leave you now." Lorenzo kissed her

lightly on the forehead. "If there's anything you need, just ring. Pina will send one of the servants up."

Ursula unpacked, gave Pina a dress to be pressed, and then, too restless to stay inside, wandered out into the garden. A mossy statue of Neptune, rising from a large fish pond, presided over circular flower beds and unexpected little marble fountains. Wishing that Lorenzo were there to enjoy it with her, Ursula strolled beyond the garden, through a shadowy grape arbor, and down a rocky hill to a pure stretch of soft sand. She took off her sandals and waded in the sea, playing a child's game with the breaking waves. Unself-conscious, carefree in her solitude, she ran along the beach until the sky turned a deep dusky rose. Worried suddenly that it was getting late, she hurried back up the hill, startled to see Lorenzo standing on the promontory.

"Lorenzo," she called. "Lorenzo." His back was toward her, and the wind was obviously drowning her voice. Laughing, she ran to him and flung her arms around his neck. He turned quickly, taking her in his arms, and even before she felt the sudden thrill of his touch, his warm, sensuous lips, she knew she had made a mistake. Too late, she pulled away.

"I thought—I made a mistake. . . ."

"And I," Enrico said.

"It never occurred to me that you'd be here this weekend," Ursula went on, flustered, accusatory.

Enrico made no reply but looked past her out to the sea. The wind blew the hair back from his tanned face, and his long dark eyes held a fathomless solemnity.

"I must go back to the house now."

He let her leave, still without speaking, and Ursula's heart beat with rage. He had kissed her so sweetly, so tenderly, as if he really cared about her. The unbelievable gall, the effrontery to kiss her like that, to take advantage of her mistake. And then to dismiss her without so much as a word, a glance. She ought to have known better than to have come to Circeo again. Yet even as she raged, Ursula realized the anger was meant for herself. Why had she succumbed to his embrace? The Botticelli Men were identical; what perversity, then, made her respond so utterly to the arrogant Enrico?

"Where have you been?"

She was surprised to see Lorenzo waiting for her near the arbor.

"I've been looking for you," he said. "Ciao, Enrico, I see you've lost no time."

Ursula turned around to see Enrico following close behind her.

"Calma, 'Enzo," he said, in a low voice and walked swiftly past them both.

"I went exploring, down to the sea," Ursula began, startled at how guilty she sounded. "I ran into Enrico on the way back."

"You didn't know he was there? He didn't ask you to meet him?"

"Of course not." Ursula turned from his anxious look and suspicious tone. "I must go and change now."

"Ursula—wait. I'm sorry if I sounded—it's just that you and Enrico—"

"Let's forget it. Please."

Although it had taken Ursula some time to get ready for the evening, choosing finally a beige caftan, arranging her hair in a twist only to let it fall loose again, she was still the first to come down to the grand salotto. It was a large, austere room, and the two plush sofas at either end seemed out of place, a touch of the modern world in an ancient setting. Tall, elegantly carved chairs were placed around gilded Florentine coffee tables, but it was the immense, pink-tinged marble fireplace that held Ursula's eye. Above it was a mosaic panel of two peacocks with a war-horse between them. A portrait hung on either side, one of a knight and the other of an exquisite lady.

"I see you've met my ancestors," Lorenzo said, smiling as he entered the room. "And that is the family emblem. The peacocks represent the knight and lady. A war was in the making, so to protect their respective kingdoms they married. Thus, the war-horse—a symbol of strength in adversity."

"And did they live happily ever after?" The thoughtful, grave look in Ursula's green eyes belied her light tone.

"Happily as two turtle doves," an unfamiliar voice replied.

She turned and saw a rather stout, bearded gentleman smiling at her.

"Father, may I present Ursula Stewart."

"Delighted," the count said warmly.

"And so am I," Ursula said, relieved to find she really meant it.

The count chuckled. "What will you drink, my dear?" He walked over to a silver serving cart filled with bottles of liquor, wines, syrupy liquers, and tonics.

"What do you recommend?"

"Ah, my dear, for you, a lovely champagne cocktail, my very own invention."

Ursula lowered her eyes, remembering when it had been Enrico saying this to her.

"But perhaps you don't care for that? You see, everyone in my family has a special champagne cocktail with their own secret ingredients. I assure you that mine is the most delectable."

"So this is your friend, Lorenzo?" The countess paused in the doorway, as though to heighten the effect of her entrance. Not that she needed to, Ursula thought, admiring her tall, cool stance, the casual elegance of her long Gucci dress.

"Good evening, Mother," Lorenzo said. "I would like you to meet Ursula Stewart."

"You seem very familiar." The countess studied her with Enrico's penetrating gaze. "Have we met before? Were you perhaps with the Principessa Folinari's party at the opera last Wednesday?"

Ursula hesitated; she could hardly remind the countess of Babington's. "No," she said, blushing. "We've never met before." Too bad Enrico was missing this little scene, she thought angrily, how amused he'd have been.

"Now what is it you do, Ursula? I don't think Lorenzo has told me," the countess said, taking the drink her husband offered.

"I study at the Belle Arti. I'm an artist."

The countess raised one finely arched eyebrow. "An artist? I see. And where did you and Lorenzo happen to meet? It's not often we have a chance to entertain Americans."

I bet, Ursula thought grimly, but kept her smile steady as she said, "It's so kind of you to have me for the weekend."

"Not at all," the countess said, indicating with a gracious wave that Ursula should come to sit beside her. "Where did you say you and 'Enzo met?"

"We met at Sergio and Dino's show, Mother," Lorenzo said. "Ursula's going to be working with

Dino. She's an excellent artist. And no doubt you have heard of her father, Professor Samuel Stewart, the well-known archaeologist."

Ursula thanked Lorenzo with a grateful look.

"Ah, we're rather in the same business, your father and I," the count said.

"Really, Pompeo, sometimes you are quite vulgar," the countess told him. "You will have to excuse my husband, Ursula. He spends so much time writing about the past that he hardly remembers the proper manners for today. But where is Enrico? He should be here by now," she fretted. "Lorenzo, would you please go and tell your brother that we are waiting." It was more a command than a request.

Lorenzo caught Ursula's eye and gave her an encouraging wink as he left the room. Little comfort, Ursula thought, for one about to be left alone with the glacial contessa. But her fears were unnecessary, for after establishing with palpable disappointment that Ursula came not from fabulous New York but Boston, the countess plunged into a one-sided conversation with her husband. She obviously had as much difficulty identifying with American commoners as Enrico did, Ursula was thinking, when the latter finally came into the salon.

"Enrico, where have you been?" the countess demanded. "This is the weekend we were to talk. I had another call yesterday from Stephania's father—"

"Not now, Mother." Enrico walked over to the liquor cart and began to mix himself a drink.

"If not now, when? Signore Pettini is very anxious to know what date we have set for the engagement party. If you refuse to discuss it, then I've no choice but to make plans without you."

Enrico turned a cold look upon his mother. "I have said, more than once, that there will be no engagement party because there will be no wedding."

"*Tranquillo, figlio mio,*" the count said, putting an arm around Enrico's shoulder.

"Come let me show you my favorite painting," Lorenzo said, hastily guiding Ursula away from the others. But the contessa's voice carried across even so vast a room.

"Don't you think this kind of extreme behavior requires an explanation? You were willing to go through with the marriage last month. At least you certainly gave the bride that impression."

"What bride?" Enrico said, his voice as angry, as sharp as his mother's. "There is no bride, there will be no marriage. Stephania has accepted this. Why can't you?"

"But you said—"

"I said when we last spoke that it could not be. If you will try to remember, I said I was in love with someone else, that I could not and would not marry Stephania."

"Who is she, then? Not the film star, that cheap girl who used to be a little hotel maid?"

"No, Mother, she's no one you know or ever will know. Now let's just drop the subject." He walked away and stood by the window, looking out to the sea.

Ursula thought of their kiss on the beach, her anger now tempered with sadness. So he had been thinking of someone else. Just as he was now, staring out at the ocean, miles away, inaccessible.

"Another drink?" Lorenzo asked, watching her with an anxious expression.

She nodded, but before he had time to refill her glass, a young maid in a white uniform appeared discreetly in the doorway.

"I believe dinner is served," the countess said

and, taking Enrico's arm affectionately, the argument forgotten, or at least postponed, led the way into the dining room.

The dinner of five courses and three wines was exquisite, but Ursula hardly noticed what she ate. She was all too conscious of the countess's polite hostility, of Enrico's stiff silence, and the way Lorenzo watched her. The threads of conversation, both in English and Italian, were so banal that Ursula could hardly concentrate on what was being said. Feeling both emotionally and physically exhausted, she excused herself shortly after the coffee had been served. She was halfway up the stairs when Lorenzo came running after her.

"Ursula, I'm sorry it's been so beastly."

"Don't be silly." She forced herself to smile. "It was a lovely dinner. Really. I'm just tired."

"Tomorrow will be different. We'll go swimming. And riding. Mother has to return to Rome in the morning. Father will be busy with his book, and I think we can trust Enrico to stay out of our way."

"It sounds like you're trying to hide me from everyone."

"On the contrary, I want you all to myself."

"And so it shall be," Ursula promised, returning his good-night kiss.

The weekend passed in a rush of pleasant activity. Lorenzo took Ursula sailing and swimming, away with well-stocked picnic hampers to explore the village for signs of Odysseus and the witch, Circe. Ursula would have almost forgotten the discomfort of the first evening had it not been for the occasional and always disturbing glimpses she had of Enrico.

On the last evening, Lorenzo, Enrico, the count,

and Ursula sat over a late supper. The count, having completed the first half of his book, insisted on first one bottle of champagne and then another, until everyone had caught his high spirits.

"I would like to make a toast to Papa's book, to *The Benvoglio Lives*," Enrico said, his face lighting up in a rare smile.

"Here, here," they all cried, emptying their glasses.

"And I would like to make a toast to Enrico's work, to the Benvoglio Industries," the count cried, refilling their glasses. "Though I confess the family enterprises of this century are more difficult than any other."

"Here, here."

"And I," Lorenzo said, his eyes on Ursula, "ask you all to join me in drinking to the health of the lady I wish to be my wife."

Nine

The only person who seemed pleased by Lorenzo's sudden announcement was the count. He gave Ursula a delighted smile and emptied his glass, oblivious to the strained silence that had fallen over the table.

"Lorenzo—" Ursula began but broke off, not knowing what to say. She was dismayed that he had not spoken to her alone, further dismayed that this should be her main reaction.

"Don't you think you should wait a little longer before such an important step?" Enrico quietly asked Lorenzo. "Does Mother know you plan to marry her?"

"Her." He spoke as though she weren't even there, Ursula thought in sudden outrage. Did he really consider an American commoner such a threat to the blue-blooded Benvoglios? She glared at him, only to find he was watching her with a kind of curiosity, the way he had looked at her when they had first met.

"You hardly know her," Enrico continued.

"Meaning that you do," Lorenzo replied, paling as he looked from him to Ursula. "In any case, it's no concern of yours."

"But this is no way to act, my sons," the count said in a baffled tone.

"Surely this is something we should discuss alone," Ursula said softly. "We'll have lots of time to talk before you go back to London, won't we?"

"London?" Enrico repeated.

"Yes, of course," Lorenzo said hastily.

Ursula got up. "If you'll excuse me now," she told the old count, "I think I'll go up to my room. We're leaving very early in the morning."

Ursula, having passed a restless night, slept most of the drive back to Rome, her dreams filled with the Botticelli men. She saw herself wearing her mother's lace wedding gown in a dark, cavernous church, and by her side stood Lorenzo. The count was blessing them both, and for some reason he was marrying them. But, when she turned to kiss her new husband, she found herself looking into the mocking eyes of Enrico.

"Bad dream?" Lorenzo asked, gently waking her.

"Yes." She sat up, looking out the car window briefly and then said, "Don't you think we should discuss last night?" She hesitated. "Your proposal at dinner—if that's what it was."

He gave her a surprised look. "But there's nothing to discuss. I love you. I want to marry you. I thought you felt the same."

Ursula smiled a little at this. "Really, Lorenzo, one

doesn't decide on marriage quite so impulsively nor so independently. It's not exactly a safari you're proposing. I'm fond of you, of course." She paused. "But love? It's too soon." How could she tell him his kisses left her unmoved? Perhaps in time it might be different. "Couldn't we go on as we were?"

"Of course," Lorenzo said, taking her hand. "I won't mention the future again until you feel sure. Only please don't let the idea of my family, of Enrico, frighten you away."

"Never," she promised him, her green eyes suddenly burning bright.

Upon arriving home Ursula found a note under the door from Dino that made her forget, at least momentarily, the weekend and the Botticelli men: "Orlando Forti is very interested in your sketches of the boy. He's having a show next month, so this could be a good chance for you. Find the child and get to work."

On the bus to the Spanish Steps, she reread the note, her excitement giving way to uncertainty. But how could she ever finish in a month? And what if she couldn't find the little gypsy boy?

But Tomaso was sitting at the top of the steps, calling out to the tourists, trying to sell his friend's cheap jewelry while the older man lay in the sun drinking from a large carafe of red wine. When he saw Ursula, the little boy's face lit up with pleasure, and he remained smiling all the taxi ride to the studio.

"Benvenuto." Dino shook Tomaso's hand with ceremony. "Ah, look, my cat has come to welcome you, too."

"Che bella," Tomaso said, crouching down to

stroke the long-haired orange cat. "What's her name?"

"Giulietta. I think she likes you." Dino watched the boy for a moment and then turning to Ursula said, "I hope you're as relaxed as your model. I have only one suggestion. In the sketch we see only the frailty of his face, but what about those narrow little shoulders jutting up through his tattered shirt? It's better, I think, to make a painting of his whole figure. Get some pillows and have him sit."

So Ursula began, lightly drawing Tomaso's angular lines, his jagged, unkempt curls. Then, staring into the black eyes that gravely met her own, she drew their delicate shape, the long lashes that fell over the shadowed hollows. She executed line after line, like an architect drawing up plans, except that behind her lines stood the sharp curves of Tomaso's thin form. Lost in her work, she was no longer aware of any time or space but that of the painting.

"I thought I'd find you here," Lorenzo said, bursting into the studio. "Ciao, Dino. And this must be the famous Tomaso."

"Yes, that's me," the child said, welcoming the chance to move.

"Lorenzo, what are you doing here?" Ursula looked up from the canvas, bemused.

"Why I've come to collect you, of course. Surely you're finished by now?"

"No, I'm not finished as it happens. Go back and sit down, Tomaso," she said, herself surprised at the sharpness of her tone.

"Oh, dear, I think that reprimand was more for me than you, Tomaso." Lorenzo sat down quickly, with so comic a look of chagrin that everybody laughed.

"Ah, if only *my* visitors were so well behaved," Dino said, and handed Lorenzo several art journals.

"Here, these might interest you while you wait."

But Ursula put away her brushes only a few minutes later. It was impossible, after all, to work with Lorenzo there. He showed no interest in Dino's work, nor even the art journals, but sat perched on the edge of his chair, his gaze fixed on her. "Okay," she said, "I guess I'll call it a day."

"And so you should," Lorenzo said, happily leaping up. "It's time for dinner, and I know a little pizzeria that makes the best calzone in Rome."

"Calzone!" Tomaso echoed, his black eyes shining.

Lorenzo turned to him. "Sorry, old chap, but these calzone are only for grown-ups." He winked. "Capisci?"

"Si, si," Tomaso replied, giving a manful shrug.

"Lorenzo, really—" Ursula started to protest. But Dino quickly intervened with: "I thought you'd stay and have supper with me and the cats, Tomaso. They're very fond of chocolate ice cream, are you?"

The boy gave a delighted laugh. "Chocolate ice cream for supper?"

"Ciao, you two," Ursula said, giving Dino a grateful look. "See you tomorrow."

The winding cobblestone streets were deserted, and the breeze from the Tiber River carried voices of families sitting down to their evening meals. The sky was a deep, dusky blue, and a thin silver moon shone between the turret of a trellis-covered palazzo and the belfry of a church.

"Why so quiet, Ursula?"

"I was thinking about Tomaso. He really wanted to come with us, you know."

"Yes, *poverino*. I'd have gladly taken him along, but I thought as you had had him on your hands all afternoon you might object."

Ursula stopped and looked at him. "Me, object?

Lorenzo, you're not serious! I love children, especially Tomaso."

He took her hand. "You don't know how pleased I am to hear that. Ah, look, here's the pizzeria."

She followed him into a large tavernlike room, quite bare save for its long wooden tables with benches and six immense stone ovens behind the counter.

"Two calzone," Lorenzo called to one of the bakers.

The room was filled with the smell of freshly baked pizza dough, and Ursula, sitting down opposite Lorenzo, said, "Oh, that smells so good. I'm starving."

"I knew you'd like it here," he said, smiling proudly, filling their glasses from a carafe of red table wine. "It's a real workingman's place."

She returned his smile, marveling once again at Enrico's dissimilar twin, this unpretentious version of the Botticelli portrait.

"*Ecco!*" A young girl wrapped in a floury apron set down a thick white platter of calzone.

Ursula bit into the crisply baked pizza sandwich of tender ham and hot melted cheese. "Delicious. How did you ever find this place?"

"Just wait. I'll show you all the culinary delights of Rome. Tomorrow we'll go to Alfredo's for fettucine. And I know a little restaurant with very special minestrone like they make in Northern Italy. Thursday is traditional gnocchi day, so for lunch we'll—"

"Hold on a minute," Ursula interrupted. "I'm not on vacation," she reminded him gently. "I've not only got Tomaso's portrait to do but also my term project to finish and exams to start studying for."

"Nonsense. You're Professor Armado's prize student. The Botticelli portrait alone will put you on the

honor list. Certainly you'll have time to be with me."
He poured himself some more wine, an expression
of petulance on his face.

Troubled, Ursula reached over and laid her hand
over his. "Don't look like that. These have to be
busy days for me. Please be patient."

He smiled and held on to her hand. "Yes, I'll be
patient. It will be different once we're married. By
the way, your grandmother will come to Rome for
the wedding, won't she?"

"I thought we agreed not to rush things." She
looked at him, her green eyes steady and earnest.
"You know I don't feel ready to talk about marriage
yet."

"Si, si—we won't talk," he said, returning her look
with a wistful one. "But at least promise me you'll
think about it."

Later that night, before she fell asleep, Ursula did,
in fact, try to imagine being married to Lorenzo,
living in London. But where? Was his flat in chic
Chelsea, overlooking the Thames? Perhaps he lived
in one of those romantic little mews near Hyde Park.
And who looked after him? Would she, as Contessa
Benvoglio, find herself confronting an ancient family retainer, another Pina, or had Lorenzo adapted
himself to English life and taken on a gentleman's
gentleman? Odd that she really knew nothing about
his life in London. She smiled, thinking how his
large, spontaneous gestures extended even to conversation, making him impatient with details. Were
he an artist, she fell asleep thinking, his paintings
would be just as he saw life—broad, sweeping lines,
extravagant canvases in primary colors."

The next week at the Belle Arti was devoted to a
general review of the material that had been covered

since the beginning of the year. One half of the term grade was based on the semester project, while the other half was the average obtained from the results of the oral and written examinations. Most of the students were so busy completing their projects that very few bothered to come to the review classes. So it was with little surprise but obvious vexation that Professor Armado looked at the handful of students assembled for his class.

"Today we will be discussing the rising concern with matters of form and space in the early Renaissance paintings. Yesterday we saw that the beginning of. . . ."

Ursula, faithfully recording the professor's words, found herself thinking of Tomaso's portrait. Every afternoon she went straight to Dino's studio, where she would find the eager Tomaso already waiting for her. And while he sat on his pillow, arms around his knees, telling her about his aunt and cousins, she painted until the last light of day.

"Knowledge of Pythagoras was quite widespread among the educated classes in the Renaissance. . . ." Ursula focused for a moment on the words pouring from her pen. Suddenly she realized she'd forgotten all about meeting Lorenzo for breakfast. Poor Lorenzo, he really was being so understanding. Every evening he came to pick her up at the studio, took her out to dinner, and, knowing she needed to spend her nights studying, he brought her home early, never even asking to come upstairs.

A loud knocking silenced Professor Armado. He glared indignantly at the offending door as if his steely gray eyes could quiet the persistent sound. "Come in," he finally barked.

Ursula turned, stifling a gasp of surprise as she saw Enrico. Quickly she bent over her notebook, pretending to write, appalled at her trembling hand.

"Forgive me, Professor Armado," Enrico was saying smoothly. "I so hate to interrupt your class, but it is imperative that I speak to Signorina Stewart."

"Si, si. Go ahead, Ursula."

She collected her things, wondering what Enrico could possibly want. Had something happened to Lorenzo? But he would be the last person to carry messages for his twin.

"I'm sorry I had to take you from class," Enrico said, as the door closed behind them. "I had to speak to you." But nothing in his calm tone bespoke urgency.

"Well?" Ursula demanded. "What is it?"

"I think it would be better if we went to a café, where we could sit down and talk."

"Very well." She followed him out of the building and into the waiting Mercedes, where they sat in continuing silence while the chauffeur drove them several blocks to Canova's, an old and elegant Roman café.

"We could easily have walked here," Ursula said, as they got out of the car.

Enrico shrugged, leading the way past counters of rich sweets, through a succession of empty little tearooms, and finally out into a garden of softly murmuring palm trees and lovers. Ursula looked away from the young couples and into Enrico's impassive face.

"Would you care for a drink?" he asked, as a waiter approached their table.

She shook her head.

"Nothing?" the waiter exclaimed. "Surely the signorina wants some refreshment on such a warm day. Iced tea or perhaps granita di limone?"

"The signorina said she wants nothing," Enrico said curtly.

"I've changed my mind." Ursula smiled at the

waiter. "A lemon ice would be lovely. I don't know why I didn't think of it myself."

Enrico shifted uncomfortably in his chair. "You may bring me a whiskey," he said, dismissing the waiter with a nod.

"Rather early for whiskey, isn't it?" Ursula said coolly. "Anyway, I thought champagne was your drink."

"For a celebration, yes. But for business, whiskey."

"Oh? I don't recall having entered into any business deal with you."

Enrico smoothed a crease in the white tablecloth. "Then perhaps I should have said I also drink whiskey on unpleasant occasions."

"You've piqued my curiosity," she said, attempting nonchalance. "Would you care to fill me in?"

He looked up, fixing his brooding eyes on hers. "I've been trying to get in touch with you since I came back from Circeo. I went to your apartment, telephoned, but never succeeded in finding you." He paused.

"Well? Is that what this is about? I'm terribly flattered at your concern, but I really don't think my whereabouts are any of your business."

"You know perfectly well that's not what I mean," Enrico said impatiently. "I was trying to find you before you did something foolish. I wanted to tell you that you cannot, you must not, marry Lorenzo."

Ursula looked at the Botticelli face she had thought so beautiful, the almond-shaped eyes that once seemed to hold such promising mystery. Why had she not seen their dark secret for what it really was? How often, she wondered, had jealousy driven him to take the fate of others into his own hands?

"You are sadly mistaken, Count Benvoglio," she said, shaking her head. "You cannot tell me what to do."

"Ursula, for your own good, you mustn't even think of this marriage."

"What I think, or what I do is no affair of yours."

"It is if Lorenzo is involved. You don't know what—"

Ursula stood up, no longer able to control her anger. "We have nothing more to discuss." She turned away, her eyes clouding with tears.

"If you'd only listen to me, you'd see that I'm trying to help you," Enrico said, following her across the patio.

"Leave me alone," she cried, and fled from the café into the street, paying no attention to where she was going, wanting only to get away from Enrico and the doubts and confusion that assailed her. Had she entirely dreamed that first, chivalrous Enrico who'd rescued her handbag? For surely this man who kept implying that she wasn't good enough to marry into his noble family must be another. Poor Lorenzo, to have to contend with this underhanded behavior, to have his happiness meddled with.

But then, could she really give him happiness? In all-fairness to him she should spend more time with him, find out what her feelings really were. They must be alone together before they were driven apart. Yes, she'd ask him to take her away this weekend, even though it meant abandoning work. Certainly the future that might be theirs was more important.

"What are you doing here so early?" Dino asked, when a few moments later a nervous but resolute Ursula arrived at the studio. "Is anything wrong?"

"No, I'm all right. Just some personal problems." She bit her lip, then burst out, "I have to go away this weekend. I won't be able to work on Tomaso's portrait."

But Dino merely nodded. "That's a very good

idea." He laughed. "Don't look at me like that. There's nothing wrong with the painting. It's fresh, alive, and forceful. But to keep its vitality, and your own, I might add, a temporary separation can only be good for you both."

"You really think so?" Ursula asked, still uncertain.

"If it will assuage your guilt feelings, I'll order you to go. Seriously, I often leave one painting for another, and then I come back refreshed."

"Yes, a rest and change of place would be helpful." And to find the answers to my heart, Ursula thought, to spend long, peaceful hours with Lorenzo without Enrico lurking in the background. Yes, this is what they needed, a chance to learn more about each other, to explore their feelings.

"Well, now that that's settled, I suggest you go home and get packed. I'll tell Tomaso to be here Monday afternoon."

"Thank you so much." Ursula gave him an impetuous kiss. "You're wonderful."

Ten

Ursula held on to the railing as the hydrofoil soared across the Bay of Naples. Sea spray fell over her face, the salty drops settling in her hair and on her eyelashes as she looked toward the mist-enshrouded Isle of Capri. Small fleets of fishermen were pulling in their nets while striped sailboats raced in the path of the setting sun. Behind the hydrofoil, in its foamy trail, a dull gray ferry, brightened by the holiday clothing of its passengers, slowly plodded along, passing white yachts that lingered luxuriously at sea. Yesterday's unpleasantness had disappeared behind a thick mist, as had the port of Naples; she was entering another world and with her was Lorenzo.

"Just two minutes away," he said, leaning over the railing next to her.

"It looks so magical," she said, as the island shed its veil of fog. What had looked to be a small rocky mountain now promised to be much more. From its base of fantastically shaped rocks and grottoes rose green hills spotted with white and pink villas, the fiery reds and soft pastels of flowers.

As the hydrofoil came into port, they saw the funicular beginning its steep ascent up the mountain.

"Too bad," Lorenzo said. "It will be ages before it comes down again, but we can take a taxi."

"Couldn't we look around the marina first?"

"You won't see much more than you do now, but, of course, my darling, if that's what you wish."

Ursula gave him a grateful smile. He was so determined to please her. From the moment she had telephoned him, this had been clear. It was she who had decided where they would go and when they would leave, Lorenzo simply nodding and smiling all the while. And now here they were, away from Rome, away from Enrico.

"Augustus thought Capri was enchanted," Lorenzo said, taking her arm as they left the boat. "He said that when you saw it from afar, it seemed to be nothing more than a massive rock, but when one set foot ashore the land flourished—"

"And when he came ashore and saw a withered holm-oak suddenly burst into leaf, he knew it was an omen," Ursula said. "My father told me the story when I was a little girl."

"So good an omen that he exchanged the larger, and, at that time, more productive island of Ischia for Capri. Did your father tell you that?"

But Ursula had stopped at the side of the pier and was gazing down into the limpid green sea. "I don't think I've ever seen such a color."

"I have. It's the same as your eyes."

They continued along the sun-baked quay into the little port.

"Well, this is your grande marina," Lorenzo said,

indicating the half-empty cafés, a few cheap tourist shops, and a taxi stand where a man sat asleep, his head resting against a dented old cab. "As you see, there's not much to explore. Shall we sit down and have a drink while we wait for the funicular?"

Ursula nodded. She was happy enough to bask in the warm light of the late sun, listening to the fishermen shout to each other in their melodiously incomprehensible southern dialect as they moored their boats.

"You should hear the accents in Sicily," Lorenzo said, watching her bemused expression. "If you're used to the Italian of Rome, it's like another language."

As they sat down at an outdoor café, church bells began to ring. On and on they pealed, first from one part of the island and then another, until the whole rocky edifice above seemed to come alive with echoing sound.

"It's not the hour, is it?" Ursula asked, checking her watch.

"No, it couldn't be—they're ringing many more times than six." Lorenzo laughed. "Maybe somebody fell from the cliff."

"What an awful thought," she said, and turned to the waiter who lounged in the doorway of the café. "Why are all the bells ringing?"

"Tomorrow is the festa of San Costanza. Each day they ring to tell her we are getting ready."

"San Costanza?"

"Yes, the patron saint of Capri," the waiter said. "She performed many miracles during her lifetime. Some say she was responsible for the death of the tyrant Tiberius, and we know she started the landslide that destroyed the Grotta Oscura—the Dark Grotto."

"Come on, darling," Lorenzo interrupted. "If there's a festa tomorrow, we'd better see about finding a place to stay."

"Yes, in just a minute." She turned back to the waiter. "I've heard of the Blue Grotto but never the Dark Grotto."

"Si, si. The Blue Grotto everybody knows. Come down here in the morning, and my brother will take you there in his boat. But first there was the Dark Grotto, a very beautiful, mysterious place full of wonders and magic. When Tiberius defiled it with his most evil deeds, San Costanza destroyed it with a landslide."

"Ursula," Lorenzo said in an urgent whisper, "I thought we came here to be together."

She looked at him in surprise. "Of course we did," she said, taking his hand, "and we are."

"San Costanza took up her olive branch," the waiter continued, "and gave a tap on Monte Solaro, like this"—he struck the table with his pencil—"and the earth started shaking until it came down and covered up the Dark Grotto."

"Remarkable," Ursula said.

Lorenzo stood up. "Here's the funicular. Are you coming?"

"Of course."

Ursula followed him across the dusty road to the small station at the base of the mountain. "I'm sorry you had to sit through all that. My curiosity often gets the better of me. You were probably raised on those stories."

"Oh, I didn't really mind. In you go," he said, holding the door of the cable car open.

"Riding in this car makes me think of ski lifts," she remarked, as they slowly started up the mountainside.

"Yes. As a matter of fact, I never get into a funicular without remembering the time I went skiing in Switzerland and the cable of the ski lift broke."

"Broke? Oh, Lorenzo—were you hurt?"

"No, not I. But some others were not so fortunate." He shook his head sadly, then smiled. But look— how do you like this for a view?" he said, as they rose past tiers of vineyards and lemon groves.

"I don't think I ever really knew what breathtaking meant," Ursula said slowly. Behind them was the marina, its clear, blue green water as flat as glass but for the small ripples made by a slowly approaching ferry. Scattered below were the half-domed roofs of ancient villas and arcaded terraces evoking days of a medieval prosperity. Green olive trees covered the island, pressing against villas already half-obscured by orange and purple bougainvillaea. "But don't we go all the way to the top of the mountain?" she asked, disappointed when the cable car stopped.

"No, this is Capri." Lorenzo picked up their luggage.

"That's the main piazza," he said as they left the station and walked into the town. "Our hotel is just beyond it, but first I have to go to the *farmacia.* I forgot my shaving gear."

"Okay. I'll wait in the piazza. It looks so pretty."

But he grabbed hold of her hand. "Oh, come with me. We can go to the piazza together later on."

Ursula hesitated, recognizing the fleeting, anxious look that crossed Lorenzo's face. It was so incongruous, she thought, that a man so adventurous could still be so dependent.

"Come," he said, pulling her hand. "It's not proper that you should wait in the piazza alone. Anyway, I want everyone to see you're with me."

"And so I am," she said, falling into step with him. She did so want this to be a perfect weekend.

"This way, signorina," Lorenzo said gaily, as they left the drugstore. He led her through an alley of old houses built into the remains of a megalithic wall, down a narrow vaulted street, and finally into a walk covered with flowering plants, a unique sort of arbor. "Ecco, the Hotel Terrazzo."

Ursula looked at the great, luxurious pink villa, struck suddenly by love's ironies. Had she run away from Enrico's passion only to invite Lorenzo's?

"Come along," Lorenzo was saying, smiling at her. "We've a far better chance of getting a room if we go inside."

Taking a deep breath to compose herself, she followed him into the large oak-paneled lobby.

"Can I help you?" A beautiful middle-aged woman with a strong French accent asked.

Ursula's heart pounded as she heard Lorenzo drawl in Enrico's voice, "We'd like to be on the terrace side. My girlfriend has never been to Capri before."

The proprietress glanced at her, and Ursula felt her cheeks grow hot, knew that even her neck would be covered in a deep blush.

"I'm afraid there's nothing," the woman said, studying her chart. "No, wait. We do have a very nice room with a balcony that looks over the water."

"Good, the signorina will have that room," Lorenzo said, signing the register. "I'll take whatever else is available." He handed Ursula the guest book to sign. "Sound all right to you?"

"Perfect," she said, smiling with relief. It was even more ironic than she thought. She had taken Lorenzo away to Capri, almost as Enrico had taken her to Circeo, and now it was Lorenzo who seemed the unsuspecting, naive one.

"Here's your key," he said as the lift stopped at the second floor. "I'm right above you in room thirty-four. See you in an hour for dinner."

Ursula's room was large and beautiful and, like the lobby, paneled in oak. The bed, covered in lace, was a marvelous nineteenth-century French four-poster. She stepped out on the balcony and gazed down over the shadowy island to the now black sea. "Beautiful," she murmured aloud, and suddenly felt sad at being left alone for this first romantic moment.

The strident ring of the telephone brought Ursula back into the room.

"It's me," Lorenzo said. "I just wanted to make sure everything's all right."

"It's divine. I'm just changing for dinner. Shall I dress up?"

"Yes, we're going to a French restaurant that serves the best Caprese food."

She laughed. "That doesn't make much sense."

"Ah, but it does. Capri was once owned by the French. Even this hotel is French—passed down through generations, you know, that sort of thing. Unfortunately, I'm terrible at dates."

"How do you ever manage at Sotheby's?"

"What do you mean by that?" Lorenzo asked sharply.

"I was only teasing," Ursula assured him. He must be tired and perhaps more sensitive about his job than she knew. She quickly changed the subject. "I've got the most beautiful view. I can't wait for you to come and see it."

"Well, I'm going down to the bar now, so we might as well meet there."

"Yes, of course," she agreed, more puzzled than disappointed.

Wrapped in a long, golden gauze dress, Ursula floated into the lobby like an ethereal spirit. The color rose to her cheeks as she became aware of all the eyes turned in her direction, and she hurried through a beaded door into the bar.

"Buona sera, signore," she said to Lorenzo, who sat hunched over his drink. He had, with his hair tumbling over his forehead, a vulnerable, strangely preoccupied look, and Ursula felt responsible and somehow guilty.

"A penny for your thoughts," she said lightly, perching herself on the stool next to him.

"Funny you should say that," he replied, straightening up and smiling. "There's a fantastic casino on the west side of the island. Why don't we go there for a few games before dinner? It would be great fun."

"Oh, Lorenzo, I'm much too hungry. I don't think I could concentrate, not even on backgammon. We can do it another time."

"Not even a quick game to whet your appetite?"

"But my appetite doesn't need whetting. Why are you so anxious to throw your money away? Isn't that Enrico's specialty?"

"I just thought you might enjoy it. It's a beautiful place, the Capri Casino. But then," he said, offering Ursula his arm, "so is the Ristorante Colette."

The warm air was scented with jasmine, and as they strolled through a maze of Moorish streets, Ursula felt at peace, as tranquil as the island night. The restaurant, built on the cliffside, was larger and more elegant than any of the other restaurants Lorenzo had taken her to.

"I'm going down to the wine cellar myself," he said, as soon as they had been shown to a window table, whose silver and crystal were reflected in the glass. "I want to get you the best bottle of champagne they've got."

Watching him leave, his handsome face lit up with enthusiasm, Ursula told herself how fortunate she was to have somebody like him care for her.

"Will you order now, mademoiselle" the waiter asked. "Or will you wait for monsieur?"

"I'll wait," she replied, and amused herself studying the other diners. One in particular held her attention, a distinguished-looking man, whose leonine head and rather thin, long nose were very familiar. She automatically reached in her purse for a pencil and began sketching his features on the back of the menu. Where had she seen him before? Was it that long-ago summer with her father in Greece?

"What are you doing?"

She glanced up into Lorenzo's angry face.

"I leave you for two minutes and look at you."

"What's wrong, Lorenzo?" She had never seen him like this, couldn't imagine what she had done to upset him.

"Isn't it enough that you spend all your time with classes, that you're constantly at Dino's with your little Tomaso? Must you be so obsessive here?" he demanded, pointing to her drawing. "I thought you wanted to come to Capri to be with me."

Ursula stared at him in surprise.

"Well, haven't you come here to be with me?"

"Yes," she said, cringing with embarassment. "Please sit down. Of course we came here to be together. I was only sketching while you were gone." She felt like a governess placating a querulous child. "But you've got to remember I am an artist, and I think that way. Surely you of all people understand that? That man seemed familiar—I was sketching him to help me remember where I had seen him before."

"So it's the man that interests you."

"Lorenzo, be quiet, for God's sake. What is wrong with you? You're not acting like yourself. How much have you had to drink?"

"Another face that fascinates you," he went right on with his tirade. "Are you tired of this Botticelli face already? Or is it because it's the wrong one? Oh, please don't pretend to be surprised. Do you really think I'm unaware of the way you felt about Enrico?"

"Stop it!"

"I suppose that old fellow over there is just as irresistible as Enrico. Yes, dear heart, another playboy of the world. Just your cup of tea."

Ursula could bear it no longer. Slowly rising to her feet, she stood in front of him, silent for a moment, and then gave him a hard slap. She stared at his surprised face, at the red mark her hand had left, and then rushed from the restaurant. No longer feeling tranquil, she raced through the streets, back to the hotel.

In her room she began pacing, not in anger but in profound dismay. How had it all begun? What had really caused this terrible and uncharacteristic outburst of Lorenzo's? Ursula searched for the answers. She regretted slapping him and, as the evening wore on, began to blame herself. It was she, after all, who had suggested this weekend, and, from his point of view, it probably would seem strange that the moment he left, she started drawing another man's face. Possessiveness was often the way of people in love. Did it seem so excessive to her because she didn't yet share Lorenzo's feelings?

125

Guiltily, she telephoned his room, but there was no answer. Every fifteen minutes she tried again, wishing she had not run away, leaving him like that. Finally at midnight, when she was getting ready to go to bed, there was a knock at the door.

"Who is it?"

"It's me," Lorenzo answered. "May I see you?"

"Yes, of course," Ursula said, hurrying to open the door. "I'm sorry about what happened."

"No, it's I who should apologize. I had no right to be jealous." He stood in the hall, staring down at the floor, his shoulders slumped in dejection. "I suppose I had too much to drink."

"I understand." She searched his dark eyes, wishing she saw more.

"So it's all right?" he asked, his face still tense.

"Yes," she replied, wondering if it was.

"I brought you this." He reached behind him for a large picnic basket filled with fruit, chicken, and a bottle of champagne.

"Fantastic! I'd forgotten how hungry I was. Let's have a midnight picnic on my terrace."

"You go ahead." Lorenzo kissed her lightly on the cheek. "I've already eaten. I'll ring you in the morning."

She closed the door behind him and unpacked the hamper, surprised at her hunger; surprised at everything. What was wrong between them? Though possessive in public, Lorenzo was never really as interested when they were actually alone. He would bring her a midnight supper but not stay to share it, and just as puzzling to her was her relief that he didn't.

The bright rays of the sun woke Ursula from a dreamless sleep. Sitting up in bed, she could see the splendors of another spring day enhanced by an orchestra of hidden birds. Breathing in the sweet scent of flowers and myrtle, she watched the eiderdown clouds moving across the blue sky. One cloud looked like a jolly, fat circus lady, only to change into two round forms. Then two thin children carrying great sacks emerged, like the gypsy boys in Rome. Like Tomaso when he carried his cloth filled with junk jewelry. She jumped out of bed and ran to her suitcase, sending clothes flying as she searched for a sketch pad. Then, settling down in a chair by the window, she drew Tomaso with an ease she had never known before. His features seemed to flow out of her fingertips, as if somehow during the night, he had entered her soul. It was almost frightening. She experimented, drawing his face behind the grill of the balcony. The effect was startling—his expression was one she had never been able to capture before; his eyes held a bright excitement, but behind that elation was hopelessness, the despair of poverty. Dino was right when he said it was good to get away from a painting. If this happened with Tomaso, what about the Botticelli Man? Ursula turned to a fresh page, watching with wonder the quick confidence of her hand. Then she stopped and shuddered, for what she had sketched was not the *Portrait of a Youth*, nor even Lorenzo, but the definitive picture of Enrico. That downward turn of the lips, which had shown a tender sorrow in Botticelli's painting, here seemed to be only more of Enrico's arrogance. She looked out at the blue sky. Was Enrico always going to be there, the cloud on her horizon?

"Ursula," Lorenzo called, tapping lightly on the door. "Are you awake yet?"

"Coming," she said, putting on her dressing gown.

"I thought we might have breakfast together," he said, coming into the room. "Shall we have it here, on your terrace?"

"Lovely. Make yourself comfortable, and I'll order some coffee and croissants."

Lorenzo did not move.

"What's wrong?" She followed his gaze to her open sketchbook. "I was drawing Tomaso." She quickly turned the pages. "It was strange because suddenly it came so easily. So I tried the Botticelli youth."

"You mean Enrico, don't you?"

"No, I don't."

"Obviously you're still infatuated with him. You can't draw a face that doesn't become his." Lorenzo spoke in a monotone, only the ashen hue of his skin revealing the depth of his feelings.

"Please, Lorenzo, don't start again," Ursula said wearily. Wasn't Enrico supposed to be the jealous brother? "Are we going to have breakfast or not?"

Lorenzo stared at the floor, clearly making an effort to recover himself. "Of course we are. But perhaps you'd enjoy it more in the piazza."

"Fine. I'll get dressed and meet you in the lobby in ten minutes."

He took her hand as she turned away, kissing her palm. "I'll be counting."

The piazza presented an intriguing spectacle of island life. Though a small square, it was the center of the town, and Caprese workmen sat at café tables next to glamorous movie stars, each party unmoved by the other. The rich exchanged gossip with the poor, the famous with the infamous. People from all different walks of life met in this same place, reveling in the same sunshine.

"Is it always like this?" Ursula asked.

"What do you mean? The weather?"

"The way all these people are together. It's like the architecture here—such a juxtaposition of the primitive and the sophisticated."

"Yes, but maybe more so today since it's a holiday. Everybody will sit here until the procession comes this afternoon. Then they'll stand up."

"Not us," Ursula ventured with a mischievous grin.

Lorenzo laughed. "Why do I get the feeling that you've got the whole day mapped out?"

"Because I do. First we take the chair lift up to Anacapri. There's a little church I read about that I'd like to sketch. Then we go down to the Blue Grotto, have lunch at the marina, then come back here to catch the parade. What's wrong?"

"I wonder why you go on and on about your sketching. Can't you ever forget you're an artist?"

"Why should I want to?" Ursula asked, incredulous. "That's like saying forget who you are, forget you're alive, forget you're a woman—" She broke off helplessly.

"I only meant I want you to really be with me."

"For God's sake, Lorenzo, please stop this foolishness. I am with you. Surely you don't begrudge me a sketch of a church."

"Go ahead then, if it's so important. But I won't stay with you to be ignored." His expression was stubborn, almost defiant. "I'll find some way to amuse myself. Perhaps I'll go to the casino."

"If that's how you choose to spend your time, it's fine with me. I'll see you back here at two."

"You're really going to leave me?"

"Aren't you the one who's leaving me?" Ursula said, no longer able to hide her anger. "This is my first visit to Capri, and I want to see it. I was hoping you'd come with me, but, as you refuse, I will go alone."

Anger and disappointment dulled Ursula's senses as she walked through narrow, festive streets to the chair lift. Groups of young children gave her San Costanza's blessings as they rushed by, one little freckle-faced girl lingering behind to ask where her boyfriend was.

"I have none," Ursula replied slowly, and realized, finally, that this was really true. She had fallen in love with a Renaissance portrait and twice had tried to force this phantom lover into reality. Poor Lorenzo, so kind and generous. . . . But even if her feeling could have grown into love, it never would have worked. She was not the right woman for him. Her independence would always be at odds with his possessiveness. Surely by now this had become clear to him, too. He would have to be very blind if this sad little trip had not shown him their profound differences.

The chair lift rose high above Capri, past the fertile vineyards and little plotted farms to a barren, craggy land. Far below, etched in the changing landscape from Capri to Anacapri, was the Scala Fencia, marking what had once been the only pathway between the two towns. At the top of the narrow stairway stood La Porta della Differenza, an ancient relic of the long feud between Capri and Anacapri. Ursula jumped off the chair onto the rust-colored earth of Monte Solaro, the island's highest point. She sketched the church of San Michelle and, wandering down to another level, found a small garden blooming in the midst of dull, dry tree stumps and evergreens. The air was filled with a wild potpourri of scents, and the land seemed to belong to some other place, so different was it from the lush vegetation of Capri.

Refreshed by the landscapes and seascapes that now filled her drawing pad, Ursula went down to the marina to find a boat going to the Blue Grotto. But the marina was like a dusty ghost town. All the activity was centered around the funicular station, where crowds of people stood waiting to be carried up to Capri.

"Isn't your brother taking people out to the Blue Grotto today?" she asked the waiter at the café.

"Ah, signorina, how nice to see you again. But it's so rough." He gestured toward the choppy sea, turbulent dark waves breaking, foamy white, against the embankment. "Better to come back tomorrow."

"I must leave tomorrow," she said, sighing.

"But that's even better, for then you will have to return to Capri. You will have a very big reason to come back, no?"

"That's true," Ursula smiled, pleased at this Caprese logic.

"The procession for San Costanza starts soon," the man said, shutting the doors of the café. As if to emphasize his words, church bells began to ring as they had the day before, first separately then in harmonious unison.

"What's that?" she asked, hearing a series of explosions.

"It is the firecrackers and rockets. Come, I'll drive you back to Capri. My family is waiting for me there, and you will join the signore, no?"

He dropped her off in the main piazza, and Ursula searched for Lorenzo, pressing through the joyous crowds to the café where they had breakfasted.

"There you are. I thought you might miss it all," Lorenzo said, standing up to greet her. "How was your morning?"

"Fine, thanks. And yours?"

"Not bad, not bad at all. Ah, you're just in time. Here they come."

Over and above the noise of the crowd, Ursula heard a distant choir, tender voices carried high on the spring air. The sweet sound of singing grew closer as the first Children of Mary in their pale blue frocks rounded the corner, their tremulous high voices rising above the shouts and applause of the crowd. The band following the children burst into triumphant fanfare, and eight saintly men in long red robes came forth. A reverent hush fell over the piazza, for these men carried the gilt statue of the patron saint, San Costanza, on their shoulders. Three ancient holy men in flowing gold robes followed the statue, murmuring blessings as they swung their censers, scattering clouds of sweet incense. The procession drew to a halt on the steps of the church and faced the adoring crowd. The band repeated the chorus of the triumphal march, and, tears running down their cheeks, people embraced each other.

"Isn't it marvelous," Lorenzo said, reaching for Ursula's arm as the band broke into Caprese folk songs. "I'm glad we came, aren't you?"

But Ursula did not hear him. Beyond the line of scarlet canons, beyond the angelic faces of the little boys, stood Enrico staring right at her.

"What did you say?" she asked, quickly turning back to Lorenzo.

"I asked how you liked the festa?" he shouted above the din.

"Splendid!" She tried to lead him away from the piazza. "Shall we go somewhere to eat?"

"I know just the place—an old family favorite."

"Oh, no," she said, fearful of meeting Enrico. "Let's go to some simple place."

"But that's exactly what it is," he said, guiding her

through the crowded streets to a small outdoor restaurant overlooking the sea.

"Why, Count Benvoglio, benvenuto," a stocky, dark woman greeted them.

"Buon giorno, signora," Lorenzo said, warmly shaking her hand. "So nice to see you. Do you have a table for us?"

"Si, si. It's just like old times to have you both here again," she said gazing over his shoulder. "I still can't tell you apart."

Ursula froze as she heard Enrico's voice. "It's been a long time, signora, and I can't wait for your insalata di mare. Come along you two," he said, "Annabella and I are starving."

Ursula darted a look at the young woman on his arm. Was this the mysterious love of his life? She was small, very feminine and fragile, moving with the grace of a gazelle. Her auburn hair, thick and shining, was piled elegantly on the top of her head, and her deep blue eyes were expertly made up.

"Fancy meeting you here," Lorenzo was saying to his twin. "What brings you to Capri?"

"Need you ask?" Enrico replied, as they sat down. "My work, of course. Forgive me," he said, turning to Ursula. "You two ladies haven't met. This is my secretary, Annabella Ponti, Signorina Stewart."

Secretary indeed, Ursula thought, surprised at herself for feeling as scandalized as Nana Willa might.

"Have you been enjoying yourself, Ursula?" Enrico asked.

"Yes, it's quite wonderful here," she said in a gay voice, not her own.

"In fact, we were just saying what a pity it is we have to leave," Lorenzo said, taking a piece of bread from the basket. "We're catching the hydrofoil back to Naples this afternoon."

Ursula said nothing. There was, of course, no reason to stay on as they'd planned. The pleasure of the trip had ended already, when she had realized she could never love Lorenzo.

"I say, what time is it?" he asked.

"Nearly three," Enrico replied, giving him a long, level look.

"I'd no idea how late it was. Come on, Ursula," Lorenzo said, pulling her to her feet, "We've less than an hour to catch the boat. Have a lovely lunch, you two. Oh, I almost forgot," he called back to Enrico, "the casino is holding a note of yours. You'd better pay up old man, or all hell will break loose."

Eleven

"You mean it's over?" Lorenzo asked, staring out the train window.

"It never really began," Ursula said gently. She looked for his reflection in the window but saw only a ghostly whiteness hovering, like a recriminating spirit, above the dark landscape.

"Just because of a few careless words said in a fit of jealousy? I know very happily married couples who have far worse scenes."

"Not that, Lorenzo, don't be silly. You're kind and generous, a dear, good friend, but I don't love you." Ursula felt numb as she spoke. How many times had she recited this little speech, how many more times would she? "We've had some wonderful times together, and I hope we'll remain friends." She loathed the words she was mouthing, knowing they were no consolation to either of them, but there was no other truth.

"Latina! Latina!" the train conductor shouted as he walked down the aisle.

Lorenzo stood up. "You need time to be by yourself, and so do I." He pulled his valise down from the rack and then took her hand. "I understand what you're feeling," he said, his soft brown eyes staring into hers, "but I'm not going to give up so easily. You will be mine."

"Oh, Lorenzo, haven't you heard a word I've been saying?" Ursula sighed and pulled her hand free. "I don't love you—I just don't love you."

"Stop saying that," he snapped, and then, taking a deep breath, added, "I know you'll realize that it must be me and no one else, and I'm content to wait."

She shook her head; it was useless to try to explain again.

"I shall get off here and go on to Circeo. I'll ring you in a couple of days."

Ursula watched Lorenzo walk across the lighted platform of the small station, wondering wretchedly if she were responsible for his weary stride, the pallor that seemed to illuminate his strained face. She had treated him badly, carelessly. She was no better than Enrico, she thought, mourning the day she had first seen him, the day she had first seen *A Portrait of a Youth.* Well, at least Enrico and the countess could relax. No doubt she'd give Enrico full credit for having scared away the American artist. But what did it matter now? It was all finished. Perfect timing, too. The term project was due this week, and that would be the end of the Botticelli men, past and present.

"Ursula! My heavens, what are you doing here?" Dino asked, coming into the studio, still in rumpled pajamas, his fuzzy hair even more wild than usual.

"I got back late last night. I couldn't sleep, so as soon as it was light, I came here. Sorry to wake you. I was trying to be quiet."

"You didn't wake me. I came in here to get something, but now I forget what," he said, rubbing his eyes and yawning.

"Dino, did you try to call me last night?"

"Me?" he murmured, distracted. "Coffee, that's what it was—I was looking for a cup. No, I didn't call you, why?"

"Oh, nothing. I think my phone is on the blink." There was no point, she decided, in burdening Dino with her dreadful night, her excessive imagination. She had arrived home shortly after eleven and, too tired to unpack, had gone straight to bed. Then, on the stroke of midnight, the phone had rung, waking her. When she'd answered, there was only silence at the other end. Thinking it a wrong number, she went back to sleep. But the phone rang again at one, and again there was only silence. The same thing happened at two. She double-locked the door, bolted the windows, and put the telephone far into the corner of the closet, but still she heard it ringing every hour. As soon as the first gray light of dawn streaked the sky, she dressed and took a cab to Dino's studio. Now last night seemed like a school-girl's nightmare, indistinct and unreal.

"I'll make us coffee, but you must find your own cup." Dino smiled, waving a mug he had found behind a pile of old newspapers, then went into the kitchen.

"Coffee's ready, but you'll have to come in here," he called a few minutes later. "I can't look at anything in the studio till I've had my first cup, not even someone as pretty as you."

Ursula glanced around the room until she spotted

a cup filled with dead flowers sitting on the window-sill.

"Oh, no—not that," Dino cried, as she came into the kitchen. "I'm painting that."

"A cup of dead flowers?"

"Exactly. It's one of my symbolic works, which no one will look at once, let alone twice. What is more depressing than a cup filled with dead flowers, I ask you? A cup, not a vase. It works wonderfully well, if I do say so myself." He put it down in the middle of the table. "Here. You can use this mug, and I'll use this little bowl. Sometimes we really must go through the studio and find all the missing kitchen things."

"I can look now."

"No, now you must sit and tell me about Capri. Did you see the Blue Grotto?"

"No, alas, it was too rough. But there was a wonderful festa, and I did quite a bit of sketching—"

"Ah, about your work, my dear. I took a good look at Tomaso's portrait. I'm quite certain you can finish it in time for the show."

"Oh, I don't think it's possible," Ursula protested. "My exams are coming up, and there's so much research I still have to do—the aqueduct, the cata-combs—"

"You'll manage. The more we have to do, the more we get done. You can't give up this opportunity. Besides, I've already given your word to Orlando Forti."

"My word?"

"Your word."

She glanced at her watch. "Tomaso won't be here for hours."

"He'll be here soon enough. It's a ridiculous notion that you need him for the body. Artistic poppycock, if you ask me. You have all the lines, so go in there and work with them."

Ursula hesitated. "I did some new sketches of his face. Would you take a look later?"

"Now is all right. This is my second coffee."

Ursula went to get her sketchbook, taking the cup of dead flowers back to its place in the corner of the studio window. She felt an overwhelming sadness at seeing the strange, faded beauty of the flowers against the gray, cobweb-covered window, and she gratefully returned to the bright kitchen.

Dino slowly examined her drawings, his critical eyes lighting up wtih pleasure. "It's not necessary that I comment. It's obvious how well you understand this little gypsy boy." He turned to the next page of the sketch pad. "Hello, what's Lorenzo doing here? Ah, but no, this definitely has the look of Enrico."

Ursula nodded, embarrassed. She'd forgotten about that sketch.

"So he found you?"

"What do you mean?"

"He came by to ask me if I knew where you'd gone for the weekend."

"Really?" she asked, keeping her voice cool. She should have guessed that was the "business" that had brought Enrico to Capri. But it was incredible, his officiousness. To think that he would follow them, that he was so obsessed with saving Lorenzo from her. Well, he could rest easy now, Ursula thought, closing the pad over Enrico's face. "I'd better get back to work," she told Dino.

Her hand seemed to move faster than it ever had before as she stood at the easel, feeling the warmth of the sun shining through the skylight. She painted Tomaso's tattered shirt, the narrow ridge of his collarbone. Then, inexplicably quickly, the white morning light had turned into the golden haze of afternoon, and the boy was there.

"Ciao, Ursula."

She turned around. "When did you get here?"

"A few minutes ago, but Dino said I must be very quiet. Do you want some coffee?" he asked eagerly.

"Yes, I'd love some. What about you, do you want a glass of milk?"

"I had some with Dino. We men eat and drink together," Tomaso said, puffing out his birdlike chest with pride. "I'll bring you some espresso, and then we must go back to work, right?"

Now for the hard part, Ursula thought, as she mixed paints, trying to find a flesh tone that would match Tomaso's hands. Too dark, she thought, applying the first blend. His fingers were a golden brown but were perpetually smudged with dirt. How to make the color of the skin separate from the dirt? With her finest sable brush she began to paint the thin fingers with their ragged fingernails and perfect half-moon cuticles. She could feel her muscles knotting up with strain and tension as she labored over the canvas.

"You'd better stop now," Dino said, behind her. "The light is fading fast, and you're squinting like a blind old lady." He looked at the portrait. "Good. The hands are a little too light, but I'll show you how to fix that tomorrow."

"Do you hear?" Ursula called to Tomaso who was already halfway out the door. "Tomorrow, same time."

On her way home Ursula walked through the Piazza Santa Maria, carefully keeping her eyes averted from the restaurant where she had first seen Enrico. Instead, she watched the children playing around the fountain, bought herself some fried rice balls at a tavola calda, then continued along the cobblestone streets to the Ponte Garibaldi, where several boys stood fishing in the dark, muddy waters of the Tiber. Halfway across the bridge she stopped to watch the sun setting beyond the hills of Rome, thinking what good a day at the studio had done her. She couldn't deny still feeling upset about Lorenzo, even more so about Enrico, but the day's hard work had dimmed her troubling thoughts.

Later that evening, a persistent ringing, as though someone were leaning on the doorbell, woke Ursula from the exhausted sleep she had fallen into as soon as she had got home.

"Signorina." A heavyset dark man flashed an identity card in her face. "Polizia. I'm Captain Rossi, this is Mazzini." He shrugged at the tall man behind him, and they walked past Ursula into the apartment.

"What's happened?" she asked, startled. "What do you want?"

"Don't worry yourself—stay calm," Captain Rossi said, wandering around the room while his partner began opening closets and cupboards.

"What's all this about?" Ursula demanded.

"Here it is, Rossi." Mazzini held up the Botticelli painting.

"What are you doing?" Ursula cried, struggling to take the painting from him. "It's mine."

"That's what they all say when they're caught," Rossi said, chuckling. "Let's have a look at whatever forgeries you call your documents."

Ursula went obediently, suddenly realizing the seriousness of her predicament. She was a foreigner in this country, and these men were obviously convinced that she had stolen the Botticelli painting. She took her passport and visa from the bureau drawer and silently handed them to the captain.

"Very nice." Rossi laughed, checking the visa. "An

excellent job of forgery. You really must have some very smart friends, no?"

"I'm afraid you're making a terrible mistake. That really is my passport and visa. I'm an art student—at the Belle Arti. You can verify everything I'm telling you. This painting is my term project, a copy of Botticelli's *A Portrait of a Youth.*"

"Save it," Rossi said, taking the painting from Mazzini. "An art student." He laughed. "Do you really take me for such a fool? Come, we'll have a nice long talk at headquarters."

They waited for Ursula to get a jacket and then escorted her down the stairs and through the courtyard, where Maria stood at her door watching.

"What is it, signorina? Are you all right?" she asked anxiously, eyeing with distrust the two officers.

"It's just a little mix-up. I'm going to the police station to straighten it all out," Ursula said, trying to sound calm.

Rossi motioned her into the backseat of a waiting black Fiat, quickly getting in beside her while Mazzini sat in front, next to the policeman at the wheel.

"So the call was legitimate," the driver said, glancing at Ursula in the rear-view mirror. "Did you call the station to tell them we're bringing her in?"

"No," Rossi answered. "I thought we might stop at a bar and have a coffee first. It's going to be a long night. We can call from there."

"Shall we go to Giorgio's?" the driver asked.

"Si, si."

The car sped down the street, cutting sharp corners until it stopped at a small café.

"Come and drink your last espresso in public." Rossi grinned at Ursula.

She shook her head, wondering if she could still be asleep, so fantastic was this whole scene.

"I'll stay and keep an eye on her," Mazzini offered. "Bring me a *doppio.*"

Ursula sat staring at the plastic upholstery of the car, trying to make some sense of what was happening. Had the Botticelli portrait really been stolen from the Borghese Gallery? Did they suspect her because she had spent so much time there? It will be all right, she told herself. She'd make them call Professor Armado, and he would clear everything up.

But as they drove into the courtyard of the police station and the high iron gates clanged shut behind them, she felt the beginnings of panic. She remembered the stories Nana Willa had told her about the unjust treatment of foreigners living abroad. The young and beautiful Beverly Rushmore, who had been accused of being a terrorist because she rented a flat once used by an underground movement. And Anthony Premble, who had died in prison after waiting six months to be tried on a quite false charge of forgery. In this country one was assumed guilty until proven innocent.

"Come along, signorina. We won't get anything done if you stay in the car," Rossi said, grabbing her wrist and pulling her out into the chill night.

They crossed the dusty courtyard and went into a dim lobby, then up several flights of dark, narrow stairs.

"I can't see," Ursula said, tripping and grabbing hold of Rossi to recover her balance.

"No funny business, signorina. It's the three of us against your one." He laughed.

"Who's in charge? I must speak to somebody."

"Don't worry. The ministero is anxiously awaiting your arrival."

When they reached the fourth floor, Rossi led her down a shadowy hallway, past a number of closed doors. The floor was littered with dirty papers, old plastic cups, and cigarette butts. A thick, dank smell hung in the air, and Ursula swallowed quickly as a wave of nausea came over her. Finally Rossi stopped and tapped twice on a green door.

"Good evening." A short, plump man admitted them. "Come in. We're delighted to have you with us. Bring me the painting, Rossi, and tell me what has happened."

"May I make a phone call?" Ursula asked, her voice hoarse with fear.

"In a moment, my dear," the man said. "Such a pretty young girl," he mused, shaking his head. "No older than my own daughter. How the world changes, eh, Rossi? Now tell me what you know."

"Well, sir, Mazzini and I were here alone. Valletto and Horazio had gone to Piazza Bologna to keep an eye on that political meeting. We sent Fabrizio out to get us some coffee and food. Then the phone rings, and it was this fellow giving us the tip, you see. So I said—"

"Rossi," the ministero interrupted, "I'm afraid you are forgetting yourself. Are you sure Fabrizio didn't bring you several liters of wine?" His small eyes narrowed threateningly. "You will take the signorina next door and see that she is comfortable, then you may finish your report."

"Si, Signore Bergamo," Rosso mumbled. "I guess I'm a little tired. The baby kept me up all night with her bawling."

"Signore Bergamo," Ursula hazarded. "Please may I make a telephone call? This is a terrible mistake. I don't know what Captain Rossi means when he says there was a tip off. Has the Botticelli really been stolen from the gallery? It must be a prank, some awful joke."

"Basta—enough!" Rossi said, grabbing Ursula by the shoulder and pulling her out of the room. "I'll be the one to tell the ministero what's what."

"Let her make the call," Signore Bergamo called after them.

Rossi took her into a small, square room, where one bare bulb hung from the ceiling. A thick layer of dust covered a desk piled high with bulging folders, but Ursula saw no telephone. Had Rossi brought her to a room without one, was he going to pretend not have heard what the ministero said?

"Go ahead, make the call," Rossi said, motioning to the desk.

She pushed the papers aside, uncovering the telephone, and started to dial Professor Armado's number, fumbling in her nervousness. Counting to ten in an effort to calm herself, she dialled again.

"Pronto?" It was Signora Armado.

"Signora, it's Ursula. Is the professor there? I'm sorry to bother him, but it's an emergency."

"Oh, my dear, what's wrong? I don't expect him for another hour or so."

Briefly, trying to keep her voice steady, Ursula explained what had happened.

"You're at the station now? Unbelievable. You poor girl. Don't worry. The minute the professor comes home I'll tell him. The curator of the Borghese Gallery is a great friend of his, and they'll have you out of there in no time."

"I wouldn't try to use the phone again," Rossi warned, as Ursula hung up. "Mazzini will be right outside this door, so if you've got any brains in that pretty head of yours, don't try anything funny." He left, slamming the door behind him.

She heard a shuffling noise in the hallway, then the creaking of another door, and knew that Rossi was closeted with the ministero, incriminating her with every word he said. She stared at the light bulb as though it were a clock, trying to see the passage of time in its dimming rays. The thoughts she had been trying to keep at bay buzzed around her head like the fly circling the light. Who, who on earth would have telephoned the police with such a story? Somebody from the Belle Arti? But why? Who would have wished this on her?

Hours seemed to have passed before the door finally opened again.

"Signorina," Signore Bergamo said, coming into the room, "I'm afraid I owe you an apology. I have just spoken with Professor Armado and the curator of the Borghese Gallery. Sometimes my men are a little overzealous in their fight against crime, and they act too quickly. Rossi, get in here," he barked. "I think you have something to say to the signorina, no?"

Rossi shuffled into the room, a sheepish look on his face. "We have been mistaken, signorina. I beg your forgiveness and indulgence. I was wrong."

"It's all right," Ursula said, stiffly rising from her chair. "It seems somebody thought I was a thief, and you knew no better than to believe what you were told. I suppose I should be flattered that you thought my painting good enough to be a Botticelli." She smiled weakly. "May I have the painting?"

Signore Bergamo returned it to her and bowed slightly. "I suggest you sign it to avoid any further confusion."

Ursula nodded. "Yes, I will. In fact, I was going to. I have to give it to Professor Armado tomorrow."

"Your papers are in order, of course," he continued. "Take good care of them and remember to get

146

your visa renewed in three months. If you have any difficulties, please come and see me."

"Thank you," Ursula said. "If everything's settled, I'd like to go home."

"Of course. Captain Rossi will drive you."

"No, it's all right, really. I'd like to walk, I need some fresh air."

"Your freedom." Signore Bergamo nodded understandingly.

As the iron gates shut behind her, Ursula felt she understood the meaning of freedom for the first time. To be able to walk alone through the streets, to breathe in the fresh night air. Suddenly aware of somebody behind her, she clutched the painting and walked faster. The footsteps came closer, were louder, and she felt her throat closing up with fear. Someone was after her. She walked even faster, but the person was gaining on her. A sharp pain shot through her side, and knowing she could go no further, she hid in an open doorway, only to see that her pursuer was a little boy, a child with a satchel of books slung over his shoulder, running down the street.

Clearly her imagination had gotten the better of her, but such crazy things were happening. Last night the telephone calls, now this. Perhaps she had been foolish not to tell the police about her anonymous caller. She paused at a street lamp and looked down into the familiar face of the Botticelli Man. Enrico's dark, penetrating eyes gazed back, and fleetingly she wondered if he could have gone to these wild extremes? He knew about the portrait, and his determination to keep her from marrying Lorenzo was certainly a motive. But, no, she just couldn't believe it.

Turning into Via Bacino, she gasped as a tall, shadowy figure rushed toward her.

"Ursula, are you all right?" Lorenzo asked, panting to catch his breath.

"I'm fine. But what are you doing here?"

"I was just at the police station," he said, frowning with concern. "They said you'd been released."

"Oh, dear. What has my portiere been telling everybody?"

"Darling Ursula, I'm not everybody. I came by when I got back from Circeo to see if you wanted to have dinner. Now tell me, poor girl, what happened?"

"It's very strange," Ursula began, as if she were talking about another person. "Somebody called the police and told them I'd stolen the Botticelli painting, so they came to my flat to get me. Professor Armado cleared the whole thing up, but it was pretty frightening. I just can't figure out who would play such a wretched joke."

"If it was a joke."

"What do you mean?"

"Ursula, anyone who lives in Rome knows that when you call the police about a foreigner, it is no joking matter. Whoever did this must really want to see you deported or worse. No—" Lorenzo murmured, shaking his head. "He couldn't have done this. . . ."

"Who? Who are you thinking of—Enrico?"

"Don't look at me like that. I know it wasn't Enrico. I was with him for most of the day in Circeo. He arrived there early this morning, and we were at the beach all day. He left only once this afternoon, to make an important telephone call."

"An important telephone call?"

"Probably a date."

"Did you tell him about us—that we were no longer together?"

"No, I told him I had every intention of marrying

you. In fact, we were discussing it until he left to make his call."

"Did you come back to Rome together?"

"No, he left before me. What's all this about, Ursula? You're as white as a ghost. You can't think it's Enrico. That's ridiculous."

Twelve

Ursula's gaze crossed the classroom, lingering over each of her fellow students, but she couldn't imagine any of them having played such a trick on her. Slowly she was becoming convinced that it could only have been Enrico. He had tried before last night to keep her from seeing Lorenzo, and if poor Lorenzo had still stubbornly insisted he was going to marry her, then Enrico obviously would resort to drastic measures. She gazed out the window at the pewter grays and greens of the rainy spring day. Yes, the more she thought about it, the more guilty he seemed to be. He had lied to her from the beginning, and if her experience with him were not enough, there were all the things Lorenzo had inadvertently said. And hadn't Paola warned her about him from the start? There was really only one thing to do. She must go and confront him, tell him that he could stop this needless persecution, that she had no intention of marrying his twin.

"You'll be responsible for a general knowledge of early Roman architecture," Professor Armado was saying. "So brush up on the structure and general history of the aqueducts, the Roman Walls, the catacombs, and other points of interest. I don't say the examination board will ask about all these, but you can be sure they'll ask at least one question. Tomorrow we'll be reviewing some of the more notable Renaissance villas and palaces. Good day."

Ursula walked down the corridor, watching the other students laughing together, their faces happy and free of worry. How she envied them. Their greatest concern was the approaching exam, and it would have been hers, too, if she had never met Enrico. She felt a sharp pang as she remembered the first day she had seen him. How gauche she had been, staring like that. If only she had walked on. . . .

"Ursula Stewart to the office. Ursula Stewart to the office," an authoritative voice came over the intercom.

What could it be now? she wondered, hurrying down to the first floor. Please, God, don't let there be more trouble, not today.

"I'm Ursula Stewart," she told the man at the desk.

"There's a telephone call for you, signorina. You can take it in the other room."

"Hello?" she spoke warily into the phone.

"I'm so glad I caught you." It was Dino.

She had forgotten all about him and Tomaso. She should be at the studio at this very moment, working on the painting.

"I was afraid you'd left. Listen, Tomaso is sick. He came by earlier, but he was sneezing and running a fever, so I took him home."

"Poor thing. But I can still come and work on the background, can't I?"

"You can, of course. On the other hand, why not

spend the afternoon studying for your exams—didn't you say you still had to research the catacombs? Then tomorrow you can give extra time to Tomaso."

"Yes, I suppose that's a good idea. I'll do just that," she said, adding silently to herself—after I pay Enrico a visit.

Ursula ran across the puddled streets of Piazza del Popolo and into Via Babuino. Her feet were wet, and her hands cold with nerves. What would she say to him? Hello, I know what you tried to do to me last night, don't try again. Or: excuse me for disturbing you, but I thought you might be interested in the odd adventure I had yesterday. She felt her throat aching with tension and wondered if she would be able to speak at all. Be tough, she told herself, as Enrico's building came into sight. This man is your enemy, he's trying to make your life impossible. He had no qualms about having you thrown into the darkest, dirtiest prison in Rome. She pressed her finger to the bell.

"Who is it?" a husky-voiced woman answered.

Please don't let this be another one of his women, Ursula prayed.

"Who is it?"

"Signorina Stewart to see Conte Benvoglio."

"Have you an appointment?"

"No, but I'm here on an urgent matter."

"*Va bene.* Take the elevator to number seven. I will tell the count you are here."

The door buzzed, releasing the catch of the lock, and Ursula stepped into the mirrored lobby. The white marble floors were so highly polished their sparkle was reflected in the mirrors, along with her very bedraggled image. She tried to untangle her wet hair and brushed ineffectually at her paint-stained jeans. Enrico would take one look at her and laugh. She gave her reflection a sharp look that said—and what if he does, you're no longer in love with him, remember?

The elevator arrived into the living room of a penthouse apartment. Annabella, the auburn-haired woman of Capri, studied her through the elevator's brass grille as though she were some curious animal in a cage. She raised a delicate eyebrow at Ursula's muddy shoes, but her wide, sensuous mouth relaxed in a smile as she opened the door of the lift.

"Good afternoon, Miss Stewart," she said in careful English. "You may wait here until the count is free. He has a very full schedule today. Please sit down." She gestured to a long brown-velvet couch. "You will find some magazines on the table."

Ursula watched Annabella's slim hips sway seductively out of the room. So she was his secretary, after all. And what else? Annabella—Anna the beautiful. Did she dine with him and sleep with him, as well as make his appointments?

"The count will see you now." She was back. "Please follow me."

They walked down a long vestibule filled with paintings of the Impressionists. There was a Renoir, the soft lilacs of a Chagall, and even an early Picasso, each painting lit by small lights concealed within the frame. At least he takes an interest in Lorenzo's work, Ursula thought, as they passed an Ernst sculpture. They entered a large room filled with books, where Enrico sat behind a desk, his dark head bent over a pile of papers.

"Hello, Ursula," he said, jumping up from his chair. "Thank you, Annabella. You may leave us now." He turned to Ursula. "Won't you sit down?"

His lips curled into the hint of a smile. "Can I get you something? You look like the proverbial cat dragged in from the rain."

"I don't care what I look like," she replied, mortified by his words. "I've an important matter to discuss with you."

"Yes, so my secretary said. Perhaps you'll sit down."

"I'm perfectly comfortable, thank you."

"Well, I'm not, so please sit. You'll join me in a brandy?"

Ursula nodded stiffly. She needed this small delay to compose herself. Perhaps the brandy would help to give her courage. Why did Enrico always set her off balance like this? She watched him coming toward her with two large crystal glasses, his dark eyes unexpectedly soft—the same brown velvet as his suit.

"I suppose this spring deluge is keeping you from sketching."

"On the contrary, I'm on my way to the catacombs." She took a sip of the warm, slightly sweet liqur. "And now, do you mind if we dispense with the pleasantries and get right to the point? Dino said you were very anxious to know where I had gone last weekend. Odd that you said nothing when we met in Capri."

Enrico brushed at a lock of his dark hair, but his face remained impassive.

"Well, aren't you going to tell me why you followed me there?"

"I think you know," he said. "I was worried when I discovered you'd gone away with Lorenzo. I felt it was my duty to make sure nothing happened."

"Like a secret elopement?"

He shrugged. "Whatever."

"And were you reassured once you'd found us?"

He hesitated. "Ursula, as long as you insist on seeing Lorenzo, I cannot be, as you put it, reassured about anything."

"Is that why you came back to Rome yesterday?" she asked, her green eyes watching him gravely.

"In a matter of speaking."

"In a matter of speaking," Ursula mimicked, and suddenly let loose a torrent of angry words. "And was it in a manner of speaking that you told the police I'd stolen the Botticelli portrait from the Borghese Gallery? Clever, and it almost worked, too. A pity you always seem to be using your wits for conniving, gambling, and women." She paused to catch her breath.

"I don't think you know what you're talking about." His voice was barely above a whisper.

"Don't I? You forget I spent half the night at the police station trying to convince my jailors that I was innocent. As you see, thanks to Professor Armado, I did finally manage to get free."

"Ursula—"

"Which brings me to the irony of it all," she rushed on. "You see, while you were plotting to keep us apart, I was telling Lorenzo that I could never marry him."

Enrico raised an eyebrow.

"Please spare me your surprise. Contrary to what you think, I'm not a scheming woman looking for wealth and a title. When I marry, if I marry, it shall be for love."

"And my brother?"

"Lorenzo is my friend." Ursula lowered her eyes. "That's all he ever was. But that isn't, and wasn't, any of your affair."

"Are you quite finished?"

"Quite."

"And you really think it was I who masterminded that bizarre incident last night?"

"Not think, I know it."

Enrico stared at her, a series of unreadable emotions flickering in his dark eyes. "Then, there's little more I can say." He finished his brandy. "As you seem to have adopted the same extreme measures of the Italian police and I don't have Professor Armado to defend me, it would clearly be a waste of time to protest my innocence." He got up and walked to the door. "My secretary will see you out."

Unaccountably dismayed at the abrupt end of their interview, Ursula followed Annabella to the elevator. Of course, she ought to have anticipated Enrico's reaction; that controlled acting, the ease with which he assumed the role of a misjudged innocent. It had been silly of her to have expected even a moment's honesty from him.

Rich golden rays of sunshine streamed into the lobby, bouncing off one mirrored wall onto another like the points of a yellow sapphire. This had to be a good omen, Ursula thought, walking out into the now sunny day. The air was sweet and clean, smelling of rainwater, and the colors of the buildings seemed clearer for their recent bath. As she climbed the winding road up to the Pincio Gardens, raindrops fell on her from the cypress trees, and she welcomed them, as though they could wash away the memory of Enrico. The air, enclosed by the forest of trees, was very still and was filled with the perfume of lavender flowers that grew in random patches. It seemed strange to think of a busy city less than a kilometer away. Yet, coming to the top of the hill, to the Piazzale Napoleone I, one could look down over all of Rome, at the terra-cotta buildings, the green terraces, and the smooth white domes of the churches. Leaning over the balustrade, trying to take in every part of the picture, Ursula heard the voices of children and turned to see a circle of white-smocked schoolchildren.

"'So high and mighty did Caesar rise,'" they sang, standing on their toes, "'with the queen of the Nile, the invasion of Gaul. He spread the Roman mile and the soccer ball, promising his people they would not fall—'"

"Never, never," cried one little boy, vigorously shaking his blond curly head.

"'But when Rome grew to her greatest size,'" the others continued to sing, "'there came the piper Nero to bring its demise.'" The children laughed and fell to the ground.

"It didn't, it didn't," the chubby little boy cried.

A young nun, their teacher, came over to embrace the child. "Yes, Alfonso, Rome did fall. When Nero was emperor, the city burned down, but that was not the end. The Romans are a strong, brave people. They built the city all over again, and that's how we come to be here today."

"So Rôme didn't fall," the child persisted.

"Let's say it took a tumble," the nun said, and catching Ursula's eye, smiled.

Ursula returned her smile and walked on, finding herself heading toward the Borghese Gallery. It seemed appropriate somehow that she should stop there today to bid a silent farewell to the youth of the past who had so changed her present. Perhaps if she saw him one last time, it would ease the dull ache that had taken root inside her.

As she walked down the white marble corridors of the gallery, its cool timelessness enveloped her. Rain or shine, summer or winter, she thought, this place remained the same, oblivious to the world outside; a vista of a past that outshone every hope of the future. She stopped at Bernini's David, noting his smooth, graceful biceps; such a figure of man would not be seen in this day. She turned to his Apollo and Daphne—surely this sun god was more wondrous than that burning disc up in the sky. And the royalty of yesterday, she mused, standing in front of Canova's Venus. Could today's noblewomen compare to her? While the nobility paid Sergio Alessandro to paint their portraits, Canova had begged Pauline Buonaparte to pose for his Venus. Yesterday, yesterday, she sighed, and in her mind she heard Paola's remonstrance, or was it her own alter ego? *Live in the present, you cannot worship an era that is past, an age you know nothing about, except the fantasies you create.*

Ursula turned away, hurrying on to *A Portrait of a Youth*. How wrong she'd been to ever think Lorenzo looked like him. It was so totally Enrico's expression, that dark, fathomless look that hid such stubborn pride. The Botticelli Man stared back at her, with even greater intensity, an urgency almost, as though he were trying to tell her something she could not hear, would not understand.

"Goodbye, my love," She whispered. "You were the sweetest dream I ever had."

By the time Ursula got back to the Via Baccina, it was late afternoon, and the shops were reopening after the siesta.

"Signorina, signorina," the dairyman called. "I have some wonderful fresh *panna* for you today, perfect to put on fruit salad in this warm weather."

"Not today, thanks," she smiled.

"Just a dollop to put in your coffee after dinner." He held up a vat of whipped cream.

"Va bene, I'll take one *etto*." She laughed and had

not walked two steps further before the woman from the wine store intercepted her.

"Signorina," she said, holding out her arms to Ursula, "is everything okay? Last night I saw those two policemen hanging around your building."

Ursula smiled. Her neighbors had probably talked of nothing else all day. "It really wasn't anything important. Just a routine check to make sure my papers were in order."

"Ah, we have such a good, strong police force," the barber said, nodding his head in admiration.

"Yes, I remember the time my sister's cousin couldn't remember where she parked her car," the butcher said. "She asked her husband what she could do, and he was too angry to think, so he asked his friend, Claudio, who is a policeman . . ."

Ursula turned into the refuge of her courtyard only to find Maria waiting for her.

"Poverina! What was that about last night?" she asked. "Is everything all right?"

"It was nothing, and I'm just fine. How would you like some fresh panna? It would be lovely on a fruit salad." Ursula parroted the dairyman's words.

"Thank you, signorina. I just made some macedoine. I'll bring you up a bowl."

"No, Maria, not now, thanks. I have to go right out again—to the catacombs. I just came home to drop off my portfolio."

It was nearly dusk by the time Ursula got to the Via Appia, much later than she had anticipated. The road was deserted, the only sounds the shrill calls of the crickets and the whisperings of the willows. She hoped it wouldn't be too late to get into the catacombs—obviously there were no tourists out sightseeing at this hour. But the gate that held the old rusted sign for the Catacombs of Saint Callistus was open. The light of an eternal flame burned over the door, illuminating a crude etching of Christ nailed to the cross. Taking a candle from a basket beside the door, she lit it from the torch and stepped inside the largest burial grounds of ancient Rome. This is research, an assignment, Ursula reminded herself, nearly choking on the thick, musty smell of decay that closed in on her as she started down the narrow stone steps that descended four levels below. The bodies of Saint Peter and Saint Paul were once buried here, and the Scipio family. It's really nothing more than a Christian cemetery.

She stopped on the first level, where a glass coffin stood in the middle of the room with one small candle burning over it. She stood for a moment looking down at an embalmed child dressed in a bridal gown. Her black hair fell in ringlets about her golden face, and she looked like a small angel. The angel of death. All around the room were shelflike compartments filled with the dead. Ursula held her candle high to examine the walls and ceiling, and very nearly screamed. The lime walls were covered with skeletons—woman skeletons in rotting silks and muslins, soldier skeletons in bloodstained uniforms of different empires and different ages. There was a faint rustle of movement, a crunch of gravel. Had she made that sound, or was someone else here? She went back to the stairs.

"Hello," she called, and as she listened to her echo, footsteps came up behind her. She tried to turn, but two strong hands had grabbed her arms, knocking the candle to the ground and forcing her to the edge of the stairwell. "Stop it!" she cried, struggling to free herself. "Let me go!" The last sound she heard was her own futile scream as she fell into the blackness.

Thirteen

Ursula opened her eyes, convinced that she was experiencing the familiar nightmare of her childhood—lost in an infernal darkness she could not penetrate, searching for the mother she did not know. She pulled her knees up under her chin, crawling into the safety of the fetal position, and her bruised body told her it was not a dream. She sat up, wincing in pain, now fully awake and alert. Someone had pushed her down the stairs to a lower level of the catacombs. She tried to remember: there had been her own shrill scream of terror bouncing off the walls again and again, and then nothing. She sat very still, listening for sounds above. After a few moments she slowly got to her feet. Her hands stretched out before her, she stumbled in the darkness, praying she would find the stairs. She wondered what had happened to her things, her bag. It must have been a mugger. Yesterday's newspaper had featured an article about the number of thieves who stalked the ruins, waiting for unsuspecting tourists.

Her hand touched a damp wall, and she turned the other way until, at last, her fingertips met the steps. Stopping at intervals to make sure there was no one else moving, Ursula crawled up the cold stone stairs to the dim light of the first level. The child's casket, even the strangely clad skeletons lining the walls, were a comforting sight. As she paused to catch her breath, she saw her candle and handbag lying near the coffin. So it had not been money her assailant had been after. She closed her eyes in a futile attempt to block out Enrico's face. But this he couldn't be responsible for. She had told him she wasn't going to marry Lorenzo. He no longer had a reason—unless he hadn't believed her. She remembered the brutal force of the hands that had pushed her. Wouldn't she have known Enrico's touch, even had it been violent, and the musky scent of his cologne? It must have been some madman, somebody hiding out in the catacombs. . . . Ursula rushed up the final flight of stairs, only to find the heavy wooden doors locked. Had an unsuspecting watchman done this—or was it the work of her attacker?

"Help, please help me!" she screamed, hurling herself against the unyielding doors again and again, recalling all the while the deserted road, knowing that there was no one to hear her. She took a nail file from her purse, trying to force the lock until the file broke in two. "Oh, God," she wept, and again beat on the doors, crying for help until her throat was raw.

Exhaustion brought with it a false calm. If her attacker was still in the catacombs, Ursula reasoned, he would have appeared again, tried to silence her. So however ghastly this interment at least for now she was safely alone. She went down again to the first level, forcing herself to think about the catacombs she had come to study. The close, dank air was, after all, only dust and lime, like a quarry, or, more familiar still, an excavation site. Hadn't she spent her childhood playing in places identical to this? She took out her sketchbook and, with a trembling hand, began to copy the crude early Christian inscriptions that covered the walls, the childlike pictures of biblical scenes: Jonah and the whale for death and salvation; baskets of bread to symbolize the Eucharist; and the most often depicted line drawing—a fish, the symbol of Christ. Though no great works of art, they were works of love and faith, and the room seemed to hold a strange aura of calm and happiness, an absolute confidence in the peace of death.

The faint sound of footsteps from outside broke the silence in which Ursula was working. She stopped, her heart pounding with fear. Had he come back? Was it her assailant returned to finish what he had started? She sat very still, beads of perspiration covering her face. She must hide, she thought, still too frightened to move. But what if it was only the night watchman making his rounds? Still clutching her sketchbook, she crept up to the doors.

"'O sole mio,'" a man was singing, his voice growing fainter.

"Help!" Ursula cried, frantically beating the door. "Help, let me out!"

The singing stopped, the footsteps returned. *"Chi é?"* the voice inquired cautiously.

"I'm a student. Please, get me out."

There was a jangling of keys, heavy bolts being drawn back, and at last the doors opened.

"Mamma mia," said the small, very distressed watchman. "What happened? How did you get locked in? There was nobody here before." He helped Ursula out into the night, anxiously talking on. "A terrible mistake, signorina. I'm so sorry."

"It's not your fault. Somebody was hiding in the catacombs and pushed me down the stairs. I thought he was after my handbag, but nothing's missing."

"O Dio," the old watchman said, mopping his brow with the handkerchief he had started to offer Ursula. "O Dio! Are you hurt? What a disgrace. Never has such a thing happened in our catacombs. Don't worry, signorina, I will report this to the authorities. They shall hear about it first thing in the morning. Poor signorina, you must come to my house now, and my wife will fix you something to eat."

"Grazie," Ursula said, gratefully letting him lead her along the path toward a little cottage, feeling stronger as she breathed the fresh night air.

A fire was burning in the grate of the small crude kitchen, and Ursula stood by the hearth, trying to stop a sudden fit of shivering.

"Please, caro," a woman called from the next room. "Leave your muddy shoes outside."

"First a glass of nice red wine and then some hot soup," the watchman said, picking up a straw-covered flagon of wine.

"What are you saying?" A short woman with large gray eyes, her white hair falling down her back in one long plait, came into the kitchen. "Madonna!" she cried in surprise, clasping her bathrobe shut. "I didn't know we had company."

"I found the signorina locked in the catacombs," the watchman explained. "She's been there for hours. Is there some minestrone left?"

"Certo," replied his wife, glancing at Ursula with sympathy and curiosity. "But what happened?"

"Somebody mugged her, in the catacombs. Can you imagine?"

As the old man spoke, Ursula found herself unwillingly thinking of Enrico again. Just as he had been the informer to the police, so must he be guilty of this. Logic pointed its finger at him. He knew where she was going, she had told him herself, and he simply had hired a thug to do his dirty work. Sighing, she remembered how he had looked at her that afternoon. His eyes had seemed to hold an expression of pain, and in her heart she had half believed in his innocence. Those deep, dark eyes—lying eyes. She took a sip of the bitter wine, swallowing with it unshed tears. Tears for Enrico and herself. How could she, after all this, still care for him?

"Please, signorina, you must eat some of the minestrone," the woman was saying. "You'll get drunk with only the wine."

Not drunk, Ursula thought, mechanically taking up a spoonful of the thick vegetable soup, just numb.

"It's late," the watchman said, "and I don't have a car, but you can stay here with us tonight. Or can I ask my cousin to drive you home?"

Ursula shook her head, smiling. "I'm fine now, really. I can take the bus."

"If you're really sure, then I'll walk you to the bus stop."

On the way back to the city, Ursula tried to sort out her thoughts. It seemed clear now that Enrico simply didn't believe she had broken with Lorenzo, that he was determined to frighten her away from Rome. But who could she tell this to? Certainly not the police. If only Lorenzo would talk to him—explain that they really were finished. But he wouldn't, he so obviously still hadn't accepted it himself. Perhaps the only thing to do, for everybody's sake, was leave, maybe go to Germany and stay with Paola and Alberto.

Rome looked like an empty mausoleum. Not a star glimmered in the gray black night. The white ruins stood out like immense ghosts, repossessing the city that had once been their own. They rose, for the moment, omnipresent and omnipotent but acutely aware of the dawn that was lining the air above and threatening in its descent to obliterate their nightly dream.

Ursula got off the bus at the Roman Forum and slowly started walking home, not even the tranquil beauty of the ruins reviving her heavy heart. Had she unconsciously tempted Enrico into these drastic actions? If she had patiently discussed everything with him instead of taking offense and flaring up, could tonight have been avoided? She shook her head. No, there weren't any excuses, Enrico had proven himself to be ruthless—a dangerous man with neither conscience nor heart.

The bright glare of a car's headlights roused Ursula from her thoughts as she turned into her street. The lights stayed focused on her, and she jumped to the side of the street, suddenly aware that she was their target, that it was Enrico's black Mercedes speeding toward her. She threw herself against a building, covering her head with her hands as the car swerved into the wall, just missing her. Through the darkened windows, she could see him frantically trying to start the car again. He's getting ready to try again, her brain warned, but she stood immobilized with fear. Then as the motor caught, she came to life, running blindly across the street to her building. The thick fortresslike doors opened, and she fell inside the courtyard.

"Oh, my God," she sobbed into the cold cobblestone floor. He had almost killed her.

"Ursula—" Enrico's tall dark figure was standing over her.

She lay still. If she didn't answer, maybe he'd think she was already dead.

"Ursula, please speak to me." He knelt, placing a hand on her forehead.

"Get away from me," she cried hoarsely.

He bent over her.

"Get away," she screamed.

"Ursula, you're upset." Enrico spoke in his most soothing tone. "Everything is going to be all right. It's over now, it's all over."

Ursula, watching him through half-closed eyes, felt like a trapped animal. He reached in his pocket. For a gun? She put her hands over her face and fainted.

"My darling, please wake up. You're safe now. Please, Ursula, my darling." The voice seemed to be coming from miles away, through layers of fog.

"Words aren't going to bring her round, Conte. What she needs is a whiff of smelling salts. That will set her right. Here, you just stand back, and I'll show you."

The strong, bitter odor made Ursula gasp and choke. She opened her eyes. She was alive, in her own bed, in her apartment, and Maria was standing over her. "Thank goodness, you're here, Maria," she whispered, taking the portiere's hand. "I thought I was going to be killed."

"You can thank the count that you weren't." Maria stepped aside to reveal Lorenzo. No, it was Enrico, watching her anxiously.

"Help me!" Ursula cried, clutching Maria's hand. "He was the one who tried to kill me. I saw him, it was his car, and he tried to run me down again and again. Call the police!"

"She's hysterical," the woman told Enrico. "Pay no mind, Conte. She'll come around presently. But perhaps you should go into the kitchen while I calm her down."

"No, signora," Enrico said. "I must talk to the signorina. Would you leave us alone for a few minutes?"

"No, don't go, Maria," Ursula begged. "You mustn't leave me with him. He'll kill me. You must call the police. Please, listen to me, Maria." Ursula could hardly speak through her tears.

"But, signorina, there's nothing to cry about anymore. We've already called the police, and they're going to catch the man who did this to you. Everything is going to be all right now. Listen to the Conte, he has taken care of everything."

"Don't leave me!" Ursula cried. "Please . . ."

Enrico walked over to the bed and looked down at her, his face pale and drawn. "I only ask for a few moments." He put his warm hand over hers. "Then you will never have to see me again." He paused. "It may be a great shock what I'm going to tell you, but you must believe me. I never tried to harm you. I never would. If I hurt you—emotionally—when I first met you, it was only that I was a big fool and didn't yet know how very much you meant to me."

"Stop your lies, I saw you."

"But that wasn't me."

Ursula stared at him. "Not Lorenzo?" she said,

incredulous. "That's impossible. He wouldn't hurt me. He wanted me to marry him. He loves me."

"I believe he does, but when you refused to marry him, that's when things began to happen, right?"

"Yes," she replied hesitantly, remembering it was that very night the telephone had rung incessantly. "But that's no proof. We were still friends. He was helping me, trying to save me from you. He knew you'd sent the police after me yesterday. And tonight if only he'd known I was at the catacombs—" She broke off, shuddering.

"But he did know, Ursula. Dino told him."

"I don't believe you."

"I tried to warn you about Lorenzo from the very beginning."

"You tried to keep me from marrying into your family."

"That's ridiculous. I wanted to ask you myself. But by then I couldn't—"

Ursula tried to sit up. "What do you mean?"

"When I began to speak about Lorenzo, you reacted so violently, I thought you loved him. It was obvious that he was in love with you."

"Oh, my God," Ursula said, beginning to understand.

"There was nothing I could do to keep you apart, so I tried to be around, to make sure nothing happened. The compulsive lying and gambling could be dealt with, but sometimes he is unpredictable, violent, as, God help us, you now know." Enrico paused again, taking both her hands into his, his troubled brown eyes gazing deep into her own. "It's so difficult to speak about it. Since he was very young, Lorenzo has been in and out of sanitariums. When you came to my apartment, I saw things were already out of hand. I found Lorenzo checking out of his hotel, totally irrational. I brought him back to my flat, but while I was trying to locate his doctor, he got away in my car. When I found you weren't home, I called the police and then came straight here. Maria let me in. It was a miracle that I saw you coming down the street and got the door open in time."

"So you saved my life?"

"Ursula, your life is dearer to me than my own."

Fourteen

"Gypsy Boy," the famous art critic, Pietro Cortina, mused, scrutinizing the portrait of Tomaso. "Yes, that upward brush stroke works perfectly. The artist certainly shows a great deal of promise. Don't you think so, dear?" He turned to his wife, who was lost in raptures over the culinary works of the chef. "I say, Tina, can't you stop eating for a moment? If you'd been looking at this painting as you were supposed to, you wouldn't be feeling so hungry."

"I'm sorry, caro, I just felt so faint. You know how I get in crowds."

"Hungry," Pietro said, giving his wife a withering glance. "But where the devil has Orlando gotten to?" He glanced around the gallery. "Didn't he say he'd be presenting the young artist to me? Do you see him anywhere?"

"Did you hear that, Ursula?" Dino asked, squeezing her hand. "It's official now. Pietro Cortina has done even more than approve your work, he's actually praised it! Do you have any idea what this will mean? The doors have been opened for you."

Ursula smiled, wishing she could genuinely share in the excitement of the moment. Here she was at her first show, her one and only piece of work was being heralded as an overwhelming success, yet all she could feel was the emptiness deep inside her.

"Orlando, Orlando," a familiar-looking young woman cried as she pushed through the room, nearly upsetting the waiter's tray of cocktails. "Come here, caro. You must tell me about this Stewart girl."

"Do you know who that is?" Dino whispered, his eyes bright with pleasure. "Nina Buccato, the most popular reporter on television. By this time tomorrow, your name will be heard all over Rome. Next week, Italy." He looked at Ursula. "You know, for somebody who's just made an unprecedented debut in the art world, you don't look very happy."

"I don't know what's wrong with me," she lied. "I guess I won't feel right until my father gets here." How could she tell Dino what was really in her heart? That she'd been praying Enrico would come. Nothing would be right until she saw him again. He'd been constantly in her thoughts since that dreadful night when finally he had told her the truth about Lorenzo.

"I think I know what's really bothering you," Dino said. "It's that strange feeling of depression one gets when a painting is done. There's so much of you in this work. You call it *Gypsy Boy*, but, after having watched you this past week, I call it *The Troubled Heart*. Now that it's finished you feel lost."

Ursula nodded, "Yes, it's true."

"I don't know what happened to you, and I don't ask you to tell me, but ever since you came back to work last week, you've painted like one possessed. Whatever you were going through, you put into Tomaso's portrait, and maybe, just maybe, that wasn't such a good thing to do."

She gave Dino a questioning look.

"Oh, I don't mean for the painting. I mean for you. Perhaps you should have dealt with some of the things that were and, no doubt still are, troubling you."

"If only I could," Ursula murmured, remembering how she had woke that next morning expecting to find Enrico still at her bedside. But he had gone, and his absence had made that day the longest one she had ever known. She had left the apartment finally, to go to the studio, where she could give utterance to her feelings through her brush. Dino was right, she had thrown herself completely into her work. All the love, hope, and pain she had experienced, and was experiencing still, she put into Tomaso's face. His dark velvet eyes with their fiery specks of gold held the same strange blend of vulnerability and daring as did her own. His fresh young face, like hers, was shadowed with suffering, the untimely marks of pain too keenly felt.

Every night she would return to her empty apartment to confront the memories that waited there. She spent hours sitting by the telephone, praying for Enrico's call, yearning for her Botticelli Man. Dino was wrong to think she had not tried to make things right. Oh, how she had tried. She had gone to Enrico's flat, she'd called his private number, then the villa in Circeo, leaving a trail of unanswered messages all over Rome.

"Ursula, I'm so glad I've found you," Professor Armado boomed from across the room, pushing through the crowd to reach her side. "My compliments on your *Gypsy Boy.* It's an excellent piece of work. You've finally overcome your difficulty with color."

This was indeed high praise, and Ursula tried to smile, but still her eyes continued their restless search for Enrico.

"Yes," Professor Armado continued, "you have realized that the uses of color in a painting are multifold, and through the variances, you have captured both the likeness of the child and his essence." He took a cocktail from a passing waiter. "But I don't suppose you need me to interpret your painting. I can't understand how you ever found time to finish it, though. I thought you spent every free moment in communion with that Botticelli man of yours."

She looked at him, startled.

"A Portrait of a Youth. You did see the mark you got for it when you checked your exam results, didn't you? No?" the professor exclaimed. "Why, you're probably the only student who didn't. But then, you found the exams very simple, didn't you?"

"No, not really." She couldn't very well tell him that she didn't remember anything about them, thoughts of Enrico had so blurred the past week of her life. Could she go on living like this, through a haze?

"Well, your grades were excellent—top of the class. And the Botticelli portrait was quite extraordinary as well, though not nearly as good as this *Gypsy Boy.* There was something unfinished about him. Maybe it was your own uncertainty about the subject that held you back." Professor Armado chuckled. "Yes, I remember how you were badgering everyone on the staff with your questions about the man. Perhaps if you'd really known him, the portrait

174

would have the completeness that this one has, that
unity between the artist and his subject."

You don't know how right you are, Ursula
thought. If only she had trusted Enrico from the
beginning. If only she had listened to him instead of
arguing and taking offense. If only . . .

"Ah, here comes my wife."

"Ciao, cara," Signora Armado said, embracing
Ursula. "My dear, I love your *Gypsy Boy*. This is the
most exciting night. Tell me, how do you feel?"

"Unreal." Ursula answered with such alacrity that
Signora Armado burst into laughter.

"Well, just don't tell that to the critics," the
professor said. "They're hailing you as the brave
new realist. Come, darling," he said, taking his
wife's arm. "We must congratulate Dino on the
on the success of his protégée."

Ursula walked out to the entrance hall, relieved to
be left alone for a moment. Alone except for the
reflection in a mirror: green eyes dark with pain,
long hair falling loose, framing a sad face in gold.
She turned away from her image, thinking she
looked like the tragic heroine of a gothic romance.
Would her whole life be spent yearning for Enrico
and what could have been? Why hadn't he come this
evening? Why, if he loved her as he said, had he
disappeared? If only she could remember that
terrible night more clearly—had she told him how
much she loved him?

"My dear girl, my darling child," Professor Stewart said, rushing to take her in his arms. "I
thought I'd never get here."

"Me, too. But you're here now, and that's all that
matters. Perfect timing if you ask me." She smiled
through her tears.

"What an occasion, my dear," her father said,

looking into the crowded gallery. "I'm absolutely bursting with pride. I just wish your Nana Willa were here." He stepped back to look at her. "But tell me, are you really all right?"

Ursula nodded. "I'm fine, I really am." She took his arm and led him into the gallery.

"Ever since Max Hamilton told me there was no Lorenzo Benvoglio working at Sotheby's I've been worried, terribly worried. In fact, I was ready to book a flight back to Rome when that chap Enrico called—"

"Enrico telephoned you?" Ursula gripped her father's arm. "What did he say?"

"He told me everything. His family's very upset about the whole business, apparently. He sounded like a nice fellow—and, of course, he was very reassuring about you. Still, I felt terrible. I ought to have told you when I was here that I had an uneasy feeling about that Lorenzo."

"I probably wouldn't have listened. Enrico tried to warn me."

"I'd like to meet him and thank him. Is he here?"

"No." Ursula avoided his eyes. "I don't know where he is." She caught sight of a well-scrubbed Tomaso entering the room, almost unrecognizable in a neat blue serge suit with long pants. "But here's someone else I'd like you to meet."

"Ciao, Ursula. Is he your father? Have you seen my modeling?" he asked Professor Stewart eagerly.

"It's not modeling anymore," Ursula smiled. "Now it's a portrait—your portrait."

"My aunt says it's my likeness and a very good one."

"I haven't seen it yet," Professor Stewart said. "But my daughter has told me a lot about you."

"She has?" the boy asked, delighted.

"Indeed she has. Now, won't you show me your modeling?"

"Oh, yes, just come with me," Tomaso said, taking Professor Stewart's hand. "We worked very hard to make this picture—I mean portrait. Every day for such a long time we would spend all the afternoon at Dino's studio, working until there was no light left and. . . ." Tomaso's high-pitched voice faded into the hum that filled the room.

"Oh, Ursula, there you are," Dino said. "That television woman has been asking me for information about you. Mamma mia, so many questions. How old are you, where do you come from, will you finish studying at the Belle Arti, what are your plans—"

She smiled sadly. "I've been asking myself the same thing. You know, Dino, I'm thinking of leaving Italy, perhaps finishing school in Paris."

"What, are you crazy? You can't do that," he protested. "You've just made a name for yourself here. This is your home."

"Drink up, Ursula," Signora Armado said, bringing her over a glass of champagne. "There's a very striking aristocrat combing the halls for you."

Ursula's heart skipped a beat. But wouldn't Signora Armado have told her if it was Enrico? A strong, familiar perfume enveloped her as someone tapped lightly on her shoulder.

"Ursula, my dear," Countess Benvoglio said in her rich, deep voice. "I've been looking for you." She took Ursula's arm and led her away from her friends. "Let me congratulate you on this smashing debut into the art world. I should like to add that I think your strength of character is as impressive as your work, if not more so." She lowered her voice. "How are you feeling? I've been very concerned about you. We all have. I wanted to tell you personally how terribly sorry I am for all that happened. I hold myself responsible for everything. When I think how Enrico begged me to speak to you. So many times he asked me to tell you about Lorenzo, but I hesitated, I put it off. When he was with you, he seemed so well. At least, that's what I kept telling myself—and the others. And when he acted irrational, when his moods swung from one extreme to the other, I said he was drunk. I closed my eyes to the truth. He was such a good child, so sweet and gentle before his mind turned. . . ."

"It's not your fault," Ursula said, taking the countess's hand. How blind she had been about this woman. So concerned with her own pride that she hadn't seen the pain written all over that majestic face, the delicately etched lines around the eyes, the slight creases in her brow.

"We tried to help him," the countess continued, a distant look in her brilliant, dark eyes, so like Enrico's. "Taking him from one country to another, from one psychiatrist to another. And with each new doctor I told myself, this time it's worked, now he's all right. Even the count thought he was better this last time. Lorenzo had been at Doctor Kroll's sanitarium for two years, and the doctor thought he was ready slowly to begin to live in the world again. So he went to stay at our estate in Sicily, with a companion to watch over him. Everything seemed to be going along splendidly for the first few months, then suddenly he turned up in Rome."

"Countess, you mustn't upset yourself," Ursula said. "You don't have to explain these things to me. I understand, really I do."

But the contessa, in her earnest, impassioned speech, was unaware of the interruption. "Lorenzo told us his companion was called away. Enrico was worried from the beginning, but I wanted to believe Lorenzo, and so I did. It was about this time that he met you. Enrico begged me to send him back to Doctor Kroll, but I wouldn't listen. I listened to Lorenzo instead, he was always such a marvelous talker. He'd been in Sicily for months, he said, and now he felt ready to face life. He wanted to live in a real place with real people. It was easy for me to agree with all he said. And when Enrico came to me concerned about you, I said we must wait, that I would meet you and see how Lorenzo behaved in your company. When you came to Circeo, I thought he acted as reasonable as any man in love, and I left before I could be proven wrong. You see, he was in love with you. But when he realized you weren't in love with him, the thread that held him together broke and he—"

"It was my fault," Ursula cried. "Oh, Countess, I really did try."

"No, it most certainly wasn't your fault, my child."

"But how is Lorenzo now, where is he? I've been so anxious for news. I've tried to reach Enrico so many times. . . ." Ursula voice trailed off.

"He's been with his brother in Switzerland. Lorenzo had an accident that night, he was trying to get to Circeo. We took him back to Geneva to Doctor Kroll." The countess gave Ursula a warm look. "It was kind of you not to press charges. You had every right to."

"Oh, no," Ursula said. "I can't help but feel responsible—"

"Because it was Enrico you loved?" the countess asked, smiling faintly.

Ursula blushed.

"It's quite all right my dear. I've known for quite some time now. I was wondering when you'd finally face it." She laughed. "Don't look so shocked. Remember Babington's? If I hadn't seen Enrico's face, then yours would have given you both away."

"But why didn't you say anything?"

"It was your affair. And when you came to Circeo with Lorenzo, I was half hoping that you might find yourself in love with him. I thought he needed your love more. That's why I carried on so about Enrico's marriage. I was a meddling old fool, but I had to make sure Lorenzo had that chance."

"It's all right, really it is."

"You've both suffered quite enough, and I'm sorry if I was responsible for keeping you apart. But all that's over now. You love each other, and there is no reason to wait any longer."

"But where is Enrico?" Ursula could not hold back the question any longer.

"Why, I believe he's over there chatting with your father," the countess said, glancing across the gallery.

Ursula looked up and met Enrico's bold gaze, those familiar dark eyes that she had never really known before. She walked across the crowded room until they stood facing one another.

"Will you?" Enrico murmured, cupping his gentle hands around her tear-stained face, his full, sad mouth only inches away from her own.

"Yes," Ursula sighed, and watched the Botticelli Man smile at last.

ABOUT THE AUTHOR

Alexandra Blakelee was born in Connecticut, but when she was twelve, her writer parents moved the family to Rome, Italy, where they spent the next ten years. Alexandra travelled extensively in Europe, studied at the University of Tel Aviv in Israel and Keele University in Staffordshire, England, where she majored in English Literature. Her greatest loves are writing, reading, traveling, and her two Persian cats. She also likes to take long walks, ride horses, swim, and live by the sea.

CIRCLE OF LOVE

Step out of your world and enter the Circle of Love.

Six new CIRCLE OF LOVE romances are available every month. Here's a preview of the six newest titles on sale May 15, 1982:

#16 INNOCENT DECEPTION by Anne Neville (#21516-7 • $1.75)

It was a chance for Laurel to taste a life of unaccustomed luxury. But little did she realize the consequences of impersonating her glamorous, coldhearted twin sister—or how her own heart would betray her once she was thrust into the arms of Derek Clayton, her sister's estranged but wealthy husband.

#17 PAMELA by Mary Mackie (#21505-1 • $1.75)

Pamela woke in a hospital room with no memory of her past, no knowledge of her name. Her only thought was of her instant attraction to the hostile and handsome man before her. Pamela did not recall anything he told her of her past...and even worse, she felt herself plunging headlong into careless desire for this dangerously seductive man.

#18 SAND CASTLES by Alexandra Kirk (#21529-9 • $1.75)

Jason Kent always got what he wanted. And now he wanted Melissa to give up her independence and become governess to his young, motherless daughter. But could she cope with the desires which welled up in her heart when Jason was near? And could she stand to be so close to him—and watch him marry another woman?

#19 THE WISHING STONE by Jean Innes
(#21518-3 • $1.75)

Katie Boswell had no qualms about giving up her city life—no regrets about becoming her widowed aunt's young companion. But why must Aunt Vee insist on playing the matchmaker—calling upon the ancient powers of the Wishing Stone to make her dreams for Katie come true?

#20 THE TEMPESTUOUS AFFAIR
by Margaret Fletcher (#21501-9 • $1.75)

Their first meeting had been stormy; their second, a shock. But now Vivienne Scott stood beside Julian Garston—the father of the man she was engaged to marry—and knew she loved him. But no one else must ever know.

#21 CIRCLES OF FATE by Anne Saunders
(#21522-1 • $1.75)

Anita was confused. No, overwhelmed! She had come to Isla de Leyenda—The Island of Legend—to see Casa Esmeralda, her mother's ancestral home and to meet Edward. She should be happy, yet all she could think of was another man—a man she hardly knew!

CIRCLE OF LOVE

With Circle of Love Romances, you treat yourself to a romantic holiday—anytime, anywhere. Enter The Circle of Love—and travel to faraway places with romantic heroes....

21502	GOLD IN HER HAIR	$1.75
21507	ROYAL WEDDING	$1.75
21500	DESIGN FOR ENCHANTMENT	$1.75
21510	THE HEATHER IS WINDBLOWN	$1.75
21508	GATES OF THE SUN	$1.75
21509	A RING AT THE READY	$1.75
21506	ASHTON'S FOLLY	$1.75
21504	THE RELUCTANT DAWN	$1.75
21503	THE CINDERELLA SEASON	$1.75

Bantam Books, Inc., Dept. CI, 414 East Golf Road, Des Plaines, Ill. 60016. Please send me the books I have checked above. I am enclosing $_____ (please add $1.00 to cover postage and handling). Send check or money order—no cash or C.O.D.'s please.

Mr/Mrs/Miss _____

Address _____

City _____ State/Zip _____

CI-3/82

Please allow four to six weeks for delivery.
This offer expires 9/82.